Deare Keri Ann
I wish for you
Beast!
Love
Kendra Mei

Congrats!
♡
Kendra Mei

MW01699656

BEAST (SPECIAL FORCES: OPERATION ALPHA)

GSG 9 CIRO 1

KENDRA MEI CHAILYN

This book is a work of fiction. Names, characters, places, and incidents are products of the author's imagination or used fictitiously. Any resemblance to actual events or locales or persons living or dead is entirely coincidental.

© 2018 ACES PRESS, LLC. ALL RIGHTS RESERVED

No part of this work may be used, stored, reproduced or transmitted without written permission from the publisher except for brief quotations for review purposes as permitted by law. This book is licensed for your personal enjoyment only. This book may not be re-sold or given away to other people. If you would like to share this book with another person, please purchase an additional copy for each recipient. If you're reading this book and did not purchase it, or it was not purchased for your use only, please purchase your own copy.

Dear Readers,

Welcome to the Special Forces: Operation Alpha Fan-Fiction world!

If you are new to this amazing world, in a nutshell the author wrote a story using one or more of my characters in it. Sometimes that character has a major role in the story, and other times they are only mentioned briefly. This is perfectly legal and allowable because they are going through Aces Press to publish the story.

This book is entirely the work of the author who wrote it. While I might have assisted with brainstorming and other ideas about which of my characters to use, I didn't have any part in the process or writing or editing the story.

I'm proud and excited that so many authors loved my characters enough that they wanted to write them into their own story. Thank you for supporting them, and me!

READ ON!

Xoxo

Susan Stoker

For the men and women who watch over us...

CHAPTER 1

Miracle Jones should have known something was off. Very rarely was the Autobahn quiet. It was always a chaotic mess that she'd become accustomed to since arriving in Germany. But for some reason, in that moment, all she could hear was the hum of her engine and the wheels as it rolled over the smooth surface. that

To give herself some company, Miracle turned on the radio and adjusted the volume so that her head wouldn't explode. She'd been nursing a slight headache for the past few hours. It was now a dull throb in the center of her forehead and she supposed that was something to be grateful for.

It'd been a long day. From the moment she opened her eyes, after breakfast of course, she'd been nose deep in dusty books that didn't seemed to have been used in a very long time. The day was spent trying to find out what happened to Heinrik Loft, a child from Adolf Hitler's circle. She wasn't certain who he was and usually she would have just let things go and move on to what she truly was supposed to be researching—WWII. But how could she just ignore the fact someone had gone through a lot of trouble to make him disappear? Sure, Loft wasn't a part of what she had planned for her dissertation, but his named popped up a few times in her research, and then it was as if he'd fallen of the face of the earth.

It piqued her interest and even if she didn't use him in the paper, she would like to know what became of him.

Call it, curiosity.

Killed the cat, Miracle. Remember that.

Miracle grunted.

Something wasn't right. No one just vanished off the face of the earth like that, without a trace. Even since there were no computers back in the day, there should be at least a paper trail as to the whereabouts of this guy or what happened to him. Then again, there were Nazis alive and well, hiding in plain sight all over the world. But this was a child. He probably didn't know what was happening, and if he did know, he may not have understood.

Miracle had contacted eighteen people, historians and archeologists mostly, and none of them wanted to talk about Heinrik Loft. They had been friendly enough until she brought up his name and then *BAM!* Their sphincters slam shut so loudly Timbuktu must have heard.

There wasn't even a legible picture of him. All the ones she could find were so damaged there was no salvaging them. One person had gone so far as to scratch out his face in a family album Miracle had found in the archives of the *Die Bibliotek* in Bonn.

She needed to regroup.

Maybe she'd have better luck at the Stadtbibliothek or one of the many other libraries in Munich.

A bright light shone in her car as a vehicle sped up behind her. The driver honked making Miracle frown. "I'm driving here!" She screamed.

The horn blared again.

Miracle tilted her head. "Go around, asshole!" She stuck a hand out her window to motion for the idiot to pass her. "What the hell is wrong with you?"

The person only kept right on honking then swerved out of the lane then back again. Miracle glanced at her speedometer. She was already going one thirty – how much faster did this joker want her to go?

Before she could decide if she should pull out of the lane, and let him pass, or be an even bigger asshole and slow down, the car behind her rammed into the back of her vehicle.

"What the—"

He hit her again. Miracle's hand slipped on her steering and the vehicle swerved dangerously to one side before she could get it back under control. There was no way she would stop on a dark road because someone hit her from behind. She'd been told many times to make sure they were in a public place before she pulled over.

The vehicle behind her swerved to her right and she figured the driver would pass her and be on their way. Miracle was wrong. The car veered toward her, slamming into the side of her brand new car. She screamed, but the other driver didn't let up. He used his car to push her against the guardrail. The sharp sound of metal on concrete filled the air, the smell of rubbing metal caught her nose and Miracle knew she couldn't keep this up. Sooner or later she would run out of space or the wall would give and then off into a blazing disaster she would go.

Miracle screamed again while slamming her foot

on the gas, propelling her forward. The vehicle attacking her crashed into the guardrail causing sparks to fly through the air.

"How'd you like that? Douchebag!" Miracle hollered out her open window.

The anger inside her wanted Miracle to stop, wait for the jerk and slammed her car into his. But logic won out. She didn't slow down or stop, she merely kept her foot on the floor, going as fast as she could manage. They finally came to a place where a gas station was located and she pulled into the parking lot where a group of men were hanging out with their motorcycles. They didn't look dangerous—hell, they couldn't be more dangerous than the creep who just tried running her off the road.

She pulled as close to them as she could possibly get and eased to a stop. They glanced over at her and one ran over to see if she was okay. She glanced back to see the offending car, had slowed down, no doubt watching to see what she would do.

Miracle smiled. "I'm fine—*danke.*"

"Were you in an accident?" he asked. "Do you want me to call someone?"

Miracle paused to find the right words in German to tell them what she wished to convey. "*Nein.*" She shook her head then paused, conjugated a few words in her head before continuing. "I'm just not used to driving here and swung a little close to the guardrail, that's all."

"Oh okay. If you are sure you are okay."

"I'm fine. *Danke*. I just want to catch my breath."

He nodded and went back to his friends and Miracle kept her eyes on the car still waiting. After an hour, she figured it wouldn't leave so she did the one thing she swore she wouldn't do. She grabbed her phone, scrolled down and clicked send.

It took a couple of rings but then the line clicked. "M.J!" John "Tex" Keegan said, his Texan accent as real as the day was long. "What a pleasant surprise. Are you missin' your Texan already?"

Already? Miracle had spent months going from Poland to Germany for her research. But she'd gone back to Norfolk a few times. She hadn't seen Tex in almost a year since they lived in completely different states.

Miracle laughed. "Does Melody know you're in love with me?" Despite her predicament, she couldn't help herself.

"She knows. She just thinks no one else would put up with my ass." Tex laughed heartily.

"And I'm right!" Melody called from somewhere on the other side. "He can be a handful!"

"And she's right." Miracle couldn't help smiling. "Say hi to her for me, but listen, I need some help."

"Help? Hold on. Mel, pass me my laptop," Tex said. "Okay, M.J, talk to me."

"Someone just tried running me off the road," Miracle said. "They rammed me from behind and then slammed into the side of my car. I found these bikers and pulled up close to them but the car is still waiting for me on the other side of the road."

"What in the hell?" The anger in Tex's voice was no surprise to Miracle. Tex was a man who believed in helping those in need, especially those he called his friends. And when his friends called him for assistance, may God have mercy on the offending party. "Stay on the line, M.J—okay—I found you. Hang tight. I'm sending back-up."

"Back-up...Tex..."

"She's ten minutes out from your location. Don't move and don't hang up."

Miracle exhaled and glanced in the rear-view mirror. The car was still there. She'd gambled that they wouldn't attack if there was a crowd around. She caught the biker's attention and waved him over. "Um—I don't feel so well. So, I've called a friend. She's on her way—could you guys stick around until she comes?"

"Sure. We'll be right here."

Miracle nodded and rested back in her seat while her good Samaritan went back to his crew.

"M.J, who are you talking to?" Tex asked.

"The bikers. They seem nice."

"They'd better be, because I have eyes on you guys right now," Tex said. "I have ways of getting a drone to drop a missile on their damn heads."

And he could do it too. Miracle had no doubt, especially since the irritation in Tex's voice was so evident.

"No need for chemical warfare." Miracle tried for a joke.

Tex grunted.

Miracle knew if Tex wasn't a good guy he'd be a major pain in authorities' asses because he was like a computer whisperer. She'd met him before he'd lost a leg, when her brother would do special operations with him. After Curtis died, Tex kind of adopted her. He checked in on her from time to time, made sure she was okay. After he lost his leg they drifted apart. He went through a phase where he just wanted to be left alone. Thankfully it hadn't lasted. She'd missed him.

Miracle kept her eyes on the car that had become like a black cloud over her. Almost ten minutes later, a green and silver car pulled up behind her attacker's. To her surprise, before anyone came out of the new car, her attackers sped off down the road. Instead of following, the green and silver car rolled toward her.

"She should be there now," Tex said. "Green and silver police car."

"You called the cops? Tex, they were probably just trying to rob me."

"She's not just any cop, M.J. Trust me. And if they just wanted your valuables, they wouldn't have stuck around after you pulled into that parkin' lot. There's something else goin' on here and I swear to keystrokes, I'm goin' to find out."

Miracle groaned. When Tex's friends were in trouble or he thought they were in danger, he was like a dog with a bone. In another life, she could have fallen in love with John Keegan. It wasn't hard to adore him. But by the time she even opened her eyes to see what a wonderful person he was, Tex had already fallen into the friend zone, swiftly moving toward big brother status.

And then there was Melody—a woman who had fallen into the ranks of Tex's world and loved him more deeply than even Miracle could imagine anyone loving another.

Someone knocked on the side of her car and Miracle just about jumped a foot in the air. Honestly, Miracle was stunned to see it was a woman. But not just any woman—this cop was gorgeous with her dark hair tied back, serious brown eyes and lips that would make any man fall to his knees and weep.

"Hello there," the officer said. "*Sprechen sie Deutsch*?"

"Just a little—*sprichst du Englisch?*"

The police smiled at her, her mouth curling upward at the corner. "Yes. I'm Sabine Henson."

Miracle hopped from the car and exhaled. "Tex, she's here."

"All right. Tell her I'll talk to her later."

"Will do."

"He says he'll talk to you later." Miracle explained to Sabine. "I don't mean to be a bother, but that car almost killed me. I didn't know what else to do."

"And you don't know who they are?" Sabine asked, inspecting Miracle's car.

"No. I'm here doing research for my dissertation. I never thought it would be dangerous!" Miracle frowned. "I go from my apartment to the library, museums—when would I have time to piss anyone off?"

"Let me escort you home," Sabine said. "I'm sure Tex got the license plate of the car so we'll look into it."

Miracle was too shaken up to argue, but she knew she couldn't drive. Not in her current condition. Now safe, her body was finally coming down off the adrenaline high. With a sigh, she shook her head while curling her fingers into tight fists. "I-I can't drive. Hell, I can't even stop my hands from shaking."

"No need to worry, ma'am." Sabine grinned, while tipping an imaginary hat. "We here in Sankt Augustin are a full service kind of police. I'll drive you home."

The smile Sabine gave her took away Miracle's worries and she nodded. "Okay, that would be nice. Thank you."

Sabine excused herself for a bit to talk into her cell and Miracle took the time to hurry over and thank the bikers who'd watched over her. They merely grinned sheepishly at her, told her they would have done it for any beautiful lady, then proceeded to, one by one, kiss the back of her hand. Although the incident bringing her into their presence was so horrendous, she couldn't help but giggle.

"Awww, sweet-talkers."

Soon she was on her way back toward her apartment, with a strange, woman driving her car. "So—how do you know Tex?" Miracle asked more to kill the silence than anything else.

"We trained together."

"I see. He was a friend of my brother's." Miracle offered.

"Was? Tex doesn't give up on friends easily. What happened?"

"Curt, died." Miracle sighed.

"I'm sorry for your loss."

"Thank you. But, he left me Tex." Miracle smiled. "Now I seem to have been adopted by a rowdy bunch of guys, and their women, I never thought I needed but adore beyond measure."

"You mean The Wolf Pack?"

Miracle laughed. "That's what you guys call them?"

"Well, they're Wolf's team—it only makes sense to call them The Wolf Pack. But I think I'm the only one who does."

"The Wolf Pack." Miracle murmured. "I like it."

Sabine glanced at her and Miracle smiled.

"So your brother was military?" Sabine asked.

"Yeah. They used to call him Chaser."

Sabine laughed fondly. “I knew Chaser.”

“You knew my brother?”

Sabine nodded, her eyes still on the road. “Sweet guy—no one would be able to tell he could bust through doors with the best of them. I met him on one of my training stints with Wolf and his team. I was sorry to hear of his death.”

“Yeah. He was my everything. So you’re not military, yet you train with American SEALs. How does that work?”

Sabine shrugged.

Miracle chewed on her bottom lip. She knew there was something Sabine wasn’t telling her but she wouldn’t push it. Tex and his friends had their secrets, and after having her brother and Tex in her life, she learned a long time ago not to ask. Instead, she snuggled in her seat, enjoying being driven for once. As the silence crept in, her mind went back to the terror she felt as that other car smashed into hers. She’d heard somewhere that during a near death experience, one’s life flashes before their eyes. They hadn’t lied.

In that moment, Miracle had seen all the things she still had left on her list to do before she died.

Fall in love.

Sleep all day.

Dance in the rain.

Laugh until she cried.

Visit the pyramids.

See the Taj Mahal.

Travel to Bora Bora.

Hear a man say *I love you* and mean it.

Most of those things could be bought—and why not? Her parents had left her millions of dollars. The least she could do was use some of it.

The ride home didn't take overly long and by the time Sabine eased the car into Miracle's assigned spot, Miracle was feeling severely drained. She expected that to happen—after the adrenaline wore off. Sabine escorted her from the lot, up the elevator and into the unit.

Miracle sighed. "Thanks for doing this."

"*Bitte,*" Sabine replied.

It took a while for Sabine to leave her apartment. The police had checked the doors, the security system then all the windows. Miracle stood with her roommate and best friend, Liane, silently, allowing Sabine to do this. Apparently, Tex would firebomb Sabine's house if she didn't ensure Miracle was safe inside. When she was finished, Sabine turned serious, brown eyes on Miracle and Liane

"Okay, if you need anything the easiest way to get

a hold of me is through Tex," Sabine said. "I'll send someone over to take care of your car. You can't ride around with all those dents."

"You really don't have to do that," Miracle said. "I have insurance that will cover the repairs. Besides, you've done so much already."

But Sabine merely smiled and stepped through the door. "Lock up after me."

With a nod, Miracle thanked her again. She closed the door and locked it. In that moment, all she wanted to do was fall into bed. But knew Liane had questions.

"Okay," Liane said, leading her back to the sofa. "Start talking."

Miracle went through the whole story and when she was finished, Liane rolled her eyes and walked into the kitchen. "Lee? Say something."

"What in the hell do you want me to say?" Liane snapped. "We should go home."

"I'm not leaving until I get what I came here for," Miracle muttered, defiance filling her tone. "I've come too far. There's no backing out. I need the research for my dissertation."

"But you're not working on what you came here for!" Liane snapped. "You're nowhere near what you came here for! And if you're dead you can't very well present your dissertation, now, can you?"

"What are you saying?"

"I'm saying use the fucking internet like a regular person!"

"I can't do that. This probably doesn't mean anything. It was most likely a mistake—like mistaken identity."

Jesus, Miracle! You could have died!" Liane tossed her hands up. "And how in the hell can they mistake a black woman in Germany? You don't exactly blend in!"

Miracle groaned.

"You know why this is happening, don't you?" Liane pushed.

"No, I don't."

"Do I have to spell it out for you? You cannot be this clueless!"

Miracle rubbed her eyes, her head had started throbbing again and she was quickly losing her patience. "Why don't you just spit it out?"

"You're looking into Heinrik Loft!" Liane said in a hoarse whisper. "The man vanished a lifetime ago and you're going to go and dig him up! Damn it, Miracle, don't you see? His Houdini act wasn't just for shits and giggles! He, or someone he knew, wanted him gone!"

"No one's trying to kill me because of some guy from the nineteen forties."

"Oh yeah? If he was a regular guy, I'd say, sure, whatever—not true. But he was a Nazi—Miracle! For crying out loud! These men are being jailed now for war crimes. No one wants to go to prison. Do you seriously think if he's still alive and knows you're digging, he's going to let you find him?"

"No."

"No. He's going to see you dead first." Liane tossed her hands up. "You're going to have to let this go or you're going to wind up road kill."

CHAPTER 2

Miracle didn't sleep all night. Tex had called to reassure her that they would get to the bottom of whatever was going on. Miracle still didn't think it was all that serious. But, there was no way of talking Tex down.

She remained awake with Liane's words surging through her head. She couldn't believe someone was trying to kill her because of some man who was most likely long dead.

No, it had to be something else.

But, they'd waited for her, like they thought she was dumb enough to pull back on the road so they could finish the job. Obviously, they did it all on purpose, because the moment they saw Sabine's car, they left like their pants were on fire.

Tex had been right. There was some next level crap happening and she might just be in the middle of it all.

Long after she heard Liane wake up and began moving about the apartment, Miracle remained still. Her friend had been upset the night before, downright pissed off, and Miracle couldn't blame her. If it weren't for those bikers and Tex, Miracle would mostly have been road kill on the Autobahn.

But she couldn't spend the rest of her life hiding out in her room. She'd travelled from Norfolk to Canada to Poland to Germany so she could finish her research and she wasn't about to let one near death experience stop her progress.

Grunting, she shoved her feet out of bed and willed herself upright. When she was certain she wouldn't fall over, Miracle wandered into her private bathroom, used the facilities, showered then brushed her teeth. Once she was dressed in a pair of jeans and a graphic t-shirt, with *Hip Hip Hooray* on the front, she walked into the kitchen.

"I made some breakfast," Liane said without facing her.

"You're still mad at me." Miracle ignored the plate and reached for the coffeepot instead. Her instinct was to turn the damn thing to her head but third degree burns would not be cool. After finding a mug, she filled it and climbed onto one of the stools.

"I'm not mad—just—well, irritated. I'll wait a little while longer then I'm heading back to Norfolk."

"I'll be more careful." Miracle promised. "But it's a little late to change my thesis now. Maybe I should just stick with books. If I hadn't started calling people none of this would have happened."

Liane sighed. "What are we doing about tonight?"

"Tonight?" Miracle asked.

"*Gieren Nach*."

Miracle had forgotten. She frowned. "Weren't you the one just saying how I could become road kill?"

Liane tilted her head. "Yeah. If you don't leave things alone. Not if you're out living your own damn life."

"I'm not..." With all the excitement from last night, going to a strip club was the absolute last thing on her mind. She didn't want to go see some half naked men prance around, but Tex had said to keep things as normal as possible. He went on about letting the bad guys think she didn't have a care in the world but Miracle had drowned him out with her mental screaming.

Then to add to the whole issue, if she'd changed her mind about going, Liane would have more questions and worry. She sighed mentally and nodded. "We're still on, of course."

"Woo!" Liane cheered before darting across the small space to hug her. "It'll take our minds off this whole sordid mess."

"That is true." Miracle reached for her plate and popped a piece of egg into her mouth. "We'll make a night of it—get all dolled up and go watch half naked men wiggle their *boo-thangs*."

Liane blinked at Miracle. "I'm sorry, what?"

"Oh nothing."

Liane giggled. "I'm gonna go call my mom. You know how she gets if I go a week without a chat."

"Yup."

Miracle watched her friend leave then finished eating and set up the dishwasher. While it ran, she headed into their office and paid all the bills. She then passed the rest of the day peering out the window, looking up and down the street, half expecting the car from the night before to be parked out there—waiting.

The day shimmered by and soon Miracle was forced to get up and dressed for their night out. It took longer than she thought it would but soon she was standing before the full length mirror in a black dress that hugged her curves, her dark hair tied back in a simple, high ponytail then carried off the whole thing with ruby stud earrings and red lips.

The outfit was Liane's idea.

Liane walked into the room, dressed in a skin tight, blue dress that had more material on the sleeve than in the length. There was no way she would be able to sit in that thing. Miracle said nothing—with her own curves, she wouldn't be able to pull that off. Hell, a dress like that would be a t-shirt on her.

"We look hot." Liane grinned.

"There's that ego again." Miracle laughed.

"It's healthy. Now, grab your purse and let's go."

"I'm driving."

Liane groaned but handed over her keys. "The one time I forgot and got wasted. You're never going to let me live it down."

They exited the apartment and hurried along the hall to the steps. The elevator was never working so of late, they women didn't bother even checking. Since they were on the second floor, it wasn't a bad walk. "I don't feel like drinking tonight," Miracle said. "I figured if I'm driving, I'd have a stronger incentive not to drink."

"Um—not even one drink?" Liane asked.

They turned the corner and descended the last set of steps. "Why?"

"Because I kinda—sorta—bought you a private dance."

"You did what?" Miracle exclaimed, glaring at Liane.

So that's why Liane was so insistent on them going to the strip club even after the road incident.

"I said, I bought you a private dance. You know? A—"

"I know what that means!" Miracle snapped. "I can't believe you did that!"

"Listen, you haven't been laid since—since—Tutankhamun ruled Egypt so I figured it's time you have some sexy stud shaking his *thang* in your lap. You can't blame a girl for trying."

They climbed into the car and Miracle started the engine then reached for her seatbelt. "It hasn't been that long."

"Oh yeah?" Liane pushed. "When was the last time you got laid?"

"I got laid in...." Miracle blinked. "Well, it was only a few—shit—"

"Like I said—18th dynasty."

Miracle groaned as she eased the car from the spot and drove out of the underground. She hadn't even gone to look at her vehicle in the light. It would bring back too many bad memories and tonight was for girls' night. She would pretend the world was perfect so Liane wouldn't worry. "Why would you do a thing like that? You know how I feel about..."

"It's only a private dance." Liane continued. "And this place is upscale, so no weird freaky dude with BO and rotted teeth."

Miracle made a face, and though she wanted to protest, she knew she'd never win. When it came to having a good time, Laine was the queen. She worked hard and believed in equalizing everything by partying just as hard. Half the time Miracle couldn't keep up and would stay home. Clubbing had never been her thing. Other times she shut up and went along with it.

The strip club *was* high end. The bouncer wore a suit. He checked their identifications quite thoroughly. But nothing prepared Miracle for what she stepped into. The place was massive with a giant stage, plush chairs, elegant bar, and an all male staff, all dressed to impress.

As the night rolled on, one stage appearance was replaced by another. Liane seemed to be having a wonderful time but the crowd made Miracle nervous. Add to that the idea she was about to have some strange man grinding on her, made her head throb. Sure, she could decline but that would only cause another migraine inducing lecture about her need to live a little.

"Okay," Liane finally said. "Follow the hottie in the bowtie."

Miracle groaned and followed the shirtless man along a path into a separate room. She never understood the reason men wore just jeans with a bowtie but no shirt. She had to admit, he wasn't bad on the eyes, though.

"Enjoy," he said.

"Um..." But he was gone before she could say anything else.

"Ooo—kay?" Miracle muttered, pushing air out her mouth causing her lips to flutter.

Since she'd never had a private dance before, Miracle wasn't sure what she should do. Miracle wasn't blind to the awkwardness of the whole situation. In fact, her heart hammered and her palms sweat. She could pace, but then she'd just look like a rabbit in a pit of snakes. Instead, she sat in one of the beautifully decorated chairs.

A door to her left opened and a man stepped through. There was no way on God's green earth a man had a right to be that sexy. He was massive—and she suddenly wanted to climb him like a tree—er, mountain. If she had been standing, Miracle knew he'd tower over her with his tall frame and sleek muscles. This dancer had the body of a man who knew precisely how to handle his woman in bed.

Chewing on the inside of her left jaw, Miracle tried not staring but failed—miserably. His face was perfect with a proud nose, sensuous mouth and silver-blue eyes. She was pretty certain if he tried, her dancer could see clean through to her soul.

Miracle blinked and shifted in her seat, trying desperately not to stare. She was already turned on and he hadn't taken a stitch of clothing off yet.

He watched her with a slow stare that she was pretty sure burned her panties off. Instead of checking, Miracle pressed her legs together.

"Hi," she said, pushing back deeper into the chair as he stepped up, and began swaying from side to side. She was an adult. Miracle knew she could have this slice of heaven gyrating for her and not be tempted to touch, to taste, to—who was she kidding?

Oh damn!

Her mother was a good woman but had a very old fashioned way of thinking. Elizabeth Jones had taught Miracle that having unclean thoughts of a man was a sin. Elizabeth was always going to church, preaching of God's mercies and that the only man a woman should see without his clothing should be her husband. She also took it a step further—the vagina was not to be talked about. The nipples, not to be talked about and a woman's orgasm wasn't important as long as the man was taken care of.

But Miracle couldn't help herself. Having this man so close was enough to make every unholy part of her pulse. Miracle caught her bottom lip between her teeth and braced herself for what was to come.

Perhaps it was because she hadn't been with a man in—well, over four years. It wasn't like they were knocking down her door. That could be the reason she had such a strong reaction to him. It had nothing to do with the fact he'd ripped his shirt open exposing abs so tight, she was pretty sure she could do her laundry on them.

She gasped, wanting to lean forward and drag her tongue against them.

Her gaze passed over the tattoo of a rose above his heart, then a coiled snake against his left ribs. His tattoos didn't end there for around his right forearm were black bands.

Sweet Jesus how am I supposed to resist all of that?

"Don't speak English?" She asked.

He stepped away, then backed into her

"My English is actually very good," he said, his voice husky. "I'm not supposed to talk to you." He gyrated into her before stepping back to trap her in her seat by gripping the arms of it.

"Do you always do as you're told?" she asked.

That got a smirk from him. "I figured you'd much rather see me take my clothes off."

"It's kind of weird having someone naked for you and you don't know their name." Miracle eyed him. "Don't you think?"

"We've all had nights where we were with someone because—there was a little too much drinking." The dancer moved against her, slowly, sensually. "You don't know each other's name. I've heard it makes things more exciting."

Miracle decided if they were to have a fling without introductions she would feel no bad ways about it.

"It's still weird. We're not drunk."

He quirked a brow. "They call me, Beast."

Yes you are, baby.

She was about to say something else when he pressed a finger to her lips. His grey eyes met hers and she swore he was trying to tell her something. Miracle sat on her hands. That way she wouldn't be tempted to touch him back. He danced around her chair, behind her then came to stand before her again, his fingers on his belt.

"Tex told me you needed help," he said. With a flick of his wrist, the belt was undone and hanging before his groin. "Sorry I wasn't available last night. But Sabine is as good as they come."

"Hold up, you know Tex?"

Beast nodded.

"And he knows I need help. *Serious help* and he sends me Magic Mike?"

Beast smiled, a look that tugged the right corner of his mouth upward and flashed something dangerous through his thigh spreading eyes. "I couldn't just knock on your front door."

She frowned. Huffing, Miracle folded her arms.

"At least pretend you're enjoying this," he said. "There are cameras in here and I need to get a few things straight with you first."

"What should I do? Shove money into your undies?"

He tilted his head as he slowly pulled the belt from the loop and discarded it carelessly on the floor. Reaching forward, he took her hands and pressed her palms to his abs. "I saw you looking at them earlier." Beast leaned in and spoke against her ear. "It's all right to touch—for now anyway."

Miracle wanted to draw her hand back. To tell this schmuck he could go to hell. But every time she tried, her body rebelled until she dragged her fingers downward. They rippled over his hardened flesh. His pants got in the way of her exploring hands but she had to behave. That didn't stop her from wishing he'd just undo that zipper and pushed those pants off. Instead, Beast stepped away and lifted both hands to drag his fingers through his hair.

"You have a cell phone?" He asked, shaking his hips.

She couldn't think.

"*Fleur*?"

"My name is..."

He smirked.

"Yes, I have a phone." She sighed. "Look, there is no need to go Liam Neeson on anyone. I'm very sure there isn't some force out there trying to get me. I mean, how bad could it be?"

"Tex believes something isn't right and I agree with him. And until he calls off the hounds, you're stuck with me."

Miracle made a mental note to have a word with John Keegan when she could and she was going to give him a piece of her mind—a profanity laced piece.

"So, phone?"

"Yes."

"Good, when I come close again, I want you to shove it into my right pocket," Beast explained. "Then reach into my left pocket for the one there."

"I'm not giving you my phone!"

"Fleur, your phone can be tracked. You're not making this easy."

"This is ridiculous! There's no one tracking my phone."

"Please don't fight me on this," Beast said. "You'll lose."

She grunted. "Self-righteous ass."

He merely smiled. "Until we can figure out what happened last night..."

She sighed but nodded. When he danced over to her, she pretended to be caressing him and did as he asked. With the new phone, she quickly placed it into her bra and rested back in the chair, pretending she wasn't a million miles away, her fingers wrapped around Heinrik Loft's throat—if he was still alive and had something to do with all this.

It wasn't entirely his fault—if she was one of those people who gave in at a roadblock, her life wouldn't have been in danger and Tex wouldn't have felt the need to send her German Thunder who was now thrusting his hips toward her.

"There is an address programmed into it. Tomorrow at four thirty, I want you to meet me there," Beast said. "Don't be late."

"You think I'm in danger and you're going to leave me?" she asked. For the first time since she entered that room Miracle was terrified. "I thought you were here to serve and protect."

"Well, if you wish for me to serve, I suggest you buy me dinner first."

"You're going to have to trust me, *Fleur*." Beast leaned in to drag his mouth from the corner of her lips up to her left ear. "If Tex is correct and something is going on, they won't stop. We end them before they end you. Meet me tomorrow. And don't worry. You'll be safe. By the way, there's a phone number on it as well—it comes directly to me if you need anything."

With that said, Beast gathered his things and exited just as silently as he'd entered. Miracle was now left with two problems—one, someone wanted to kill her and two, she was soaking wet and Beast wasn't even gentleman enough to help her with that issue.

CHAPTER 3

Leaving the strip club by the side door, Beast stuck his ear piece in. "Barbie."

"I'm here," Barbie answered. "Did you find her?"

"Oh—he found her alright," Tex's drawl filled the earpiece.

"Tex." Beast warned.

"Damn, Beast" Tex cut in. "Didn't know you had moves like that."

Beast frowned. "You're one nosy son of a bitch, you know that?"

"Guilty as charged." Tex chuckled. "But you adore me."

"You two can make love later," Mouth said, laughter in his voice. "Right now, we need more information."

"Agreed," Beast said. "But I can't be in two places at once. Barbie, go to the *Gieren Nach* and keep an eye on them. Dress to impress."

"Fashion is my jam, you know that," Barbie said.

Beast chuckled. "Once they leave, Mouth, take over. I'll relieve you the second I can. If I can't I'll have to send Zero."

"Roger that," Mouth said.

There were a couple of clicks indicating his teammates had gone off to follow his instructions. He cleared his throat. "Tex."

"Dude was asked to help with some training at your headquarters," Tex said. "If you're running low on manpower I can have him chip in. I'm sure he won't mind."

"Wait, Dude is here?" Beast asked.

"Came in twenty minutes ago." Tex replied. "I know he isn't supposed to out on ops but—we gatta do what we gatta do."

"Don't make the call right now." Beast glanced around to ensure he was still alone. "Let us figure out if there really is an issue first. No sense sounding all the alarms just yet."

Tex agreed and after the conversation was over, Beast pulled his helmet on while shoving his thumb against the sensor to start the engine. After checking the preheated oven. When he closed the door, he set the timer then faced Zero.

"Not many people have heard of him. It's not like they taught us anything about him in school. His name was mentioned a few times but just to read over and move on. When the war ended, he just kind of vanished."

"So, he could still be alive."

"Yeah," Zero replied.

"Well, we'll look into all possibilities."

While they waited for dinner to cook, the two delved into more research. By the time the food was ready, they were right back to where they started—being as clear as mud.

The two ate in relative silence. They tried once more to figure out why Miracle was attacked while sipping on beers but in the end, they were still nowhere close to deciding if there was any real danger.

Soon, Zero called it a night and left the apartment. But Beast couldn't sleep. He checked in with Mouth and Barbie about how Miracle and her friend were doing then crawled into bed. It was useless. He should've known the sandman would be a jerk. He finally gave up and wandered back into the living room where her information sat on the center table.

Around two in the morning, his phone rang. He glanced at the screen to see *Fleur* flashing at him. He smiled, and answered it.

"Miracle, is something wrong?" he asked.

She gasped softly, her breathing hitching in her throat. "No. Nothing's wrong. I just wanted—well, I just wanted..."

."You wanted?" Beast set down the photo of her he'd been staring at and eased from the sofa. Suddenly the heat in the room was intolerable. Opened the glass door leading to the balcony and stepped through into the cool air. "Did you want me to tuck you in, *Fleur?*"

He could almost see her frowning. At the strip club she'd shown her irritation by allowing the spot between her eyes to crease, her eyes squinted then huffing. She made an irritated sound on the other end of the line and he laughed.

"That's a dumb thing to say." She muttered.

"You haven't denied it."

"And how precisely would you—you know what? Never mind. I just wanted..." She sighed in what seemed to be frustration.

"I'm only a man," Beast said. He couldn't remember a time he'd spoken so softly. "All you have to do is open your beautiful lips and let the words fall out."

"It's not that easy. Words hurt, you know?"

"And do you want to hurt me now, *Fleur*?"

She hissed at him.

"You have to tell me what you want. If you can't say it, you can't have it."

A soft whimper left her lips and he smiled. If he didn't know better, he'd think Miracle was calling to ask him for a little phone fun. Though the thought of sliding over her body in bed, taking her hard and fast to ride her until she's climaxed enough times to fall asleep was tempting, Beast bit his tongue.

"I couldn't sleep and I figured I could talk to you."

"Okay." Beast settled into his seat. "What did you want to talk about?"

"Do you really think I'm in trouble?"

"Well, I won't speculate until I figure who owns that car. Miracle, why did you *really* call me?"

"I don't know."

."Listen, I know this isn't the ideal situation," Beast said, entering the room and closing the door behind him. He pulled the curtains in place then flopped back onto the sofa. "But we'll do what we can to get you out of here safely."

"Liane too?"

"Liane—I was..." Beast stopped himself. "Yes. Liane too."

"Should I keep calling you Beast?" Miracle asked. "It would be nice to know your real name."

Beast hesitated but then remembered the phone was secure. He smiled. "Alric. My name is Alric Gerhart."

"Alric—not what I expected."

"Oh?" Beast asked. "What did you expect? Bob?"

.Miracle laughed, a smoky sound that left him trembling.

"Good night, Beast," she said.

"Goodnight, *Fleur.*" His voice cracked but he waited until he heard dial tone before he hung up.

Sweet dreams.

It had been nice speaking to Beast on the phone. And afterward, Miracle spent a few minutes thinking of the heat in his tone and the wetness between her legs. She wouldn't feel guilty for that, no matter what her mother's ghost was telling her. After all, Miracle was a woman—and women notice when a man as fine as Beast did anything, right? She would have to be dead to not be turned on by him.

Then again, they didn't see him half naked and gyrating or feel his tight abs ripple under their palms. Put all of that together and Miracle wanted to explode.

Besides, would it be so bad to have Beast touch her—just once?

She fell asleep with a smile.

The next morning, Miracle was thrust back into reality when the magnitude of what had truly happened returned.

She paced her bedroom wondering if she should stay in that day. There wasn't really anything she *needed* that couldn't wait until after her get together with Beast. But why should she hide away? Sure, Miracle appreciated the fact that she might be in danger but what was she supposed to do? Live the rest of her life in her apartment?

No, she wasn't about to be a shut in.

She'd just pulled on her jeans when her laptop beeped and Melody's face popped onto the screen.

"Jesus!" Miracle exclaimed. "I could have been naked, you know?"

Melody laughed. "I told him so. That's why Tex had me call first. How are you, Miracle?"

"I've been better. You're glowing."

Melody laughed. "How can I not be? I have a sexy as hell man, who loves me and friends who are fantastic—a pain in the butt sometimes, but fantastic."

"One day I want all that."

"And you will. I hear Beast isn't exactly bad looking."

"Hey!" Tex said, sticking his head into view. "None of that."

Melody and Miracle laughed. Melody blew her a kiss, dropped one to the side of Tex's head and rose from the chair. After she was gone, Tex's eyes became serious.

"Listen, I've been doing some diggin'," Tex said. "I haven't called Beast yet but I'm goin' to have to."

Feeling the air suck out of the room, Miracle picked up her laptop and moved to the bed. She curled her legs under her and focused on Tex's handsome face. "Okay. I'm sitting. Let's have it."

"I found out you've been asking questions on Heinrik Loft. I went back into all the information I found and dug a little deeper into that name. After World War 2 ended, he went underground for a while. Surfaced when he was twenty-one and tried reviving Hitler's old ideals. It didn't pan out and he fell off the grid again. In Germany, he has a group that is still loyal to him. They operate in silence and are quite deadly. They haven't really been that serious until two years ago they started makin' some noise."

"Is he alive?"

"If he is, I haven't been able to find anythin' on him. No credit card, phone bills, bank accounts, tax returns—nada. But, they don't call me the computer whisperer for nothin'. It's gonna take me a bit—especially since if he's alive, he's using an alias. But I'll find him."

"So they really are after me."

"I'm afraid so, my beauty. But don't worry. I know Beast and his team and they are some of the best. Plus, Dude is in that neck of the woods."

"Faulkner is here?"

"Yeah. M.J, I'm not gonna lie to you. These guys are dangerous. They set off an explosive outside a preschool two years ago because they learned the Chancellor's son was enrolled there. This is no joke. I don't want you takin' any unnecessary risks."

"What am I supposed to do then? Just wither away in this apartment? I can't go back home because then I would have failed my dissertation and..."

"Miracle, you're a billionaire—why is this so important right now—in this very moment in time?"

"You wouldn't understand. Thanks for your help but I have to go."

"Miracle!"

But she closed the laptop with a quick flip of a wrist and left the bedroom. Though Liane asked her what was happening, she said nothing of her talk with Tex. Just the mere thought of it made her sick to her stomach. And the last thing she wanted was another damn lecture. There were so many things running around in her head as she left Liane in the apartment and made her way down to her car. When she reached it, Miracle was stunned to see the damage to the side was no longer there. Glancing around, she pulled out her cell and called Beast.

"Miracle. What's up?"

"Did you fix my car?" She asked, opening the door and sliding into the leather seat.

"Mouth has a friend who fixed your car," Beast replied. "Do you like it?"

"Yes. You have to thank him for me," Miracle said. "But you guys didn't have to do that."

"You are familiar with how this little family works, correct?" Beast asked. "We do for each other."

Miracle smiled. Cookie, one of Tex's friends, had

told her the same thing on the day they laid Curtis to rest.

She thanked Beast again.

"Where are you going, *Fleur*?"

"I had a life before all this bullshit, remember?" Miracle said. "I'm going to pick up a few things." She wouldn't tell him she was going to buy pepper spray, since it might be illegal in Germany.

Beast laughed. "Lingerie?"

"I didn't think a man with the name Beast would want lingerie. I figured you'd just want easy access."

"Lingerie is always a good thing, Miracle—they sound beautiful being ripped from the body."

Miracle bit back a whimper and pressed her legs together. "I have to go!" She hung up quickly and dropped the phone on the passenger seat. Shaking it off, she drove from the parking space and headed into the center of the city. She'd always planned on getting some new jeans and underwear. If she went about her life as usual, all she had to do was be careful.

At the mall, she stopped for a coffee then got into getting the things she needed. Usually, she'd spend hours, window shopping and the like. But knowing some strange organization was out to get her, quickened her steps and the length of her transactions.

She'd just stepped out of the final store when she was bounced on both sides. Arms grabbed her shoulders and something hard was shoved into her side.

"No screaming," a man's gruff voice warned. "Any sound and you're dead."

CHAPTER 4

Beast moved along the second story, keeping his eyes on Miracle. The way she walked into the stores and the speed of her exits told him she was nervous. Though his job was to protect her, Beast couldn't ignore the fact she was sexy. Everything from her cool, dark skin, to the curve of her body and the sway of her hips with each step— all of it told him she was the kind of woman he could have some fun with. She was the type of woman who would let him tear her lingerie from her body and not be angry about it.

God, I hope you are.

When she dipped into a particular store, Beast knew she didn't exactly go for clothes. That store had been known to supply women with pepper spray for protection. Pepper spray was technically illegal but law enforcement looked the other way most often than not. Around the precincts, they would rather the woman ward off an attacker than having to explain to her family why she wouldn't be coming home anymore.

"Bad girl," Beast muttered.

The pleasure I would gain from punishing you...

The moment she was grabbed he knew it and all thoughts of anything carnal vanished. Though everyone else around moved about their day, he quickened his steps. He could go back down the steps but there was a chance he'd lose sight of them and people could get in his way. No, Beast had to go in from above.

Keeping his eyes on the three, he pushed his way over to the railing and climbed up. He timed it, then leapt through the air, landing on top of the guy holding Miracle's right arm. The shock of it caused the other man to release her and while kneeling into the down man's neck, Beast lifted a high kick into the other's chin. With the second attacker stunned, Beast slammed his captive's face into the tiled floor just as a painful growl filled the air. Beast looked up to see that Miracle had somehow gotten the other man's arm behind him and each time he moved, she would shift a little to his left, twisting his arm painfully.

Pride further soared as she kicked him hard in the back of the knees making him fall face first to the tile. Beast rose and took him off her hands, tossed him on top of the other man and led her out of the mall.

"Where's your car?" He asked.

"On the other side of the building," Miracle said.

"Good. We're going to leave it there for now. I think there's a tracking device on it. I'll have Pitbull take care of it. Come with me."

"How did you find me?" Miracle asked as they jogged toward his Jeep.

"Do you seriously think you were alone?" Beast asked.

He saw the frustration on her face but didn't address it. Instead, he pressed the remote on his keychain and allowed her to climb into the passenger side of the jeep before making his way around to the driver's side. At that moment, one of the men staggered out the entrance of the mall and began looking around. Beast didn't move, didn't start the ignition. The last thing he wanted to do was draw attention to them. He assumed this guy was looking for Miracle's car.

"We need information," Beast said.

"What are you thinking?"

"His buddy is probably still unconscious." Beast glanced around. The parking lot was empty except for vehicles. "We're going to take him."

"What? Are you insane?"

Beast didn't reply. He merely pulled a Glock 17 from his waist and checked the chamber. After taking off the safety, he pressed into her hand. "Have you ever fired one of these?"

"Once—Beast."

"Put it in your purse. I'm sorry, *Fleur* but I'm going to use you as bait."

Miracle nodded. "I can do this."

"Yes, you can," Beast cradled her face. He glanced over to see the man was now speaking on his phone. "I want you to get out of the jeep and walk in a straight line. Don't look back until I call you."

"Got it."

"I won't let anything happen to you—I promise."

Beast leaned in and kissed her forehead. He wasn't even sure why he did that but it was an overwhelming urge he couldn't deny even if he tried. He released her and exited the vehicle then watched as she did as he instructed. Beast waited until the aggressor saw Miracle. When the man went after her, Beast moved quickly and quietly and before the attacker even knew what was happening, Beast was behind him and had him in a sleeper hold. Within seconds, the man's body became heavy in Beast's arms and his pulse weakened.

"Miracle!" Beast called.

She stopped and jogged back to him as he threw the man over his shoulder and they headed back to the jeep. Beast tossed the man into the trunk then went through the man's pockets. Beast took his phone and everything else the man carried that might hold a tracking device. He ripped the buttons off the man's shirt and pants, patted him down just in case they'd sewn something into the lining of his clothing then felt along his arm for implanted devices. Not finding any, he handed everything he'd confiscated to Miracle to dump into a nearby garbage can.

"Get in." Beast advised her when she returned. He slammed the trunk shut. "It's going to be a long —long day."

On the way back, Beast accepted his Glock from Miracle and holstered it. He stopped and dropped his captive off to Mouth and Zero. "Find out what he knows," Beast said. "I don't care how you do it."

Mouth nodded while slipping cuffs on the captive. "Did he go after Miracle?"

"Yes," Miracle said. "There's another guy but I think his face was bashed in."

Zero arched a brow.

"I'll take this guy to lock up," Mouth said and led their captive off.

"We'll find out what he knows." Zero promised.

"Thank you," Beast said. "Listen, have Barbie head back to her apartment and get Miracle's friend some protection. We all know how these guys work."

"On it," Zero said.

Beast managed to get Miracle back into the Jeep but she was silent now. He knew, from experience that wasn't a good sign. When he got her back to his apartment, Beast watched her fall into the sofa and pressed her face into the cushion. She screamed a couple of times then went silent. Beast sat beside her on the edge of the sofa and touched her shoulder.

"*Fleur*?"

"Why do you call me that?" Miracle lifted her head. "You're not French."

"I was brought up in an orphanage that was run by French nuns," he explained. "I speak English, French, and German fluently. As well as a little Japanese I learned from Zero."

"And calling me flower..."

"A flower is very beautiful, Miracle. That's why I call you that."

She turned onto her back and relaxed onto the sofa. "Does this mean you think I'm beautiful?"

Beast smiled. He didn't want to seem unprofessional but what man could resist those eyes, those lips, those breasts. "Yes."

His mind and control slipped further when she pressed her palm against his belt buckle then dragged her fingers up his clothed chest to stop between his pecks. Fire trailed after her hand, burning Beast sweetly. He touched her shoulder, dragged his palm up and down her arm until he cupped the side of her face. Almost in a trance, Beast bowed forward, closed his eyes and held his breath until their mouths met. At first, he merely pressed his lips to hers, feeling their suppleness and the way they trembled against his. Her breath, hot against his face aroused him making him tingle. But then she spread her lips, giving him control and access and Beast growled. He plunged into her heat, seeking her tongue. When he found it, Beast sucked it into his mouth before flicking his tongue around it.

Miracle moaned and tangled her arms around

his neck, and it was his total undoing. She deepened the kiss to his pleasure, reaching for the front of his shirt. But Beast caught her fingers and pulled back, panting.

"What's wrong?" Miracle asked, her voice breathy.

"We have to stop." Beast explained as he bowed his head and kissed her fingers. "I want to—so bad, but I can't."

Miracle dragged her hands away and turned her face to the back of the sofa. He caught her chin between two fingers. Beast turned her head so their eyes could meet as he took one of her hands and brought it down to the front of his pants. He splayed her fingers against his hardness and pressed.

"Do you feel that, *Fleur*?" Beast asked, hovering his mouth over hers. "Does that feel like a man who isn't completely aroused by you?"

Miracle shook her head.

"Trust me on this, Miracle, nothing would give me greater pleasure than to have you naked and panting under me. To see and feel your beautiful breasts fill my palms and taste your nipples tighten against my tongue. But my pleasure isn't the most important thing right now. Here's the deal. First, I save your life, then I make your body burn."

She trembled but said nothing.

"I know you like the sound of that." Beast passed a hand down her neck then to cup a breast. He found her nipple through the soft material of her clothing and flicked at it with his nail until she was arching up into his hand. "Do we have a deal, *Fleur*?"

"Beast..." she whispered.

"I want one simple word from you, *Fleur*." Beast trailed his hand downward and with a quick flick of his fingers, he undid the button on her jeans then pushed the zipper down. He snaked the fingers into her panty and was proud to feel it wet. But his mission was simple. He found her entrance and slid his finger in. Beast fingered her while watching her face, loving the expressions that passed over her beautiful features. Miracle caught her bottom lip between her teeth as her eyes rolled back.

"Alric, oh, damn."

She dug her nails into Beast, something that hardened him even more. He wished he could remove his shirt and felt her nails bite into his flesh. This was just for her—to show her how desperately he wanted her.

"Tell me what you want, Miracle," Beast said, withdrawing the finger and adding a second before slipping them into her.

"Make me—make me come."

"That's my girl," Beast whispered.

To give her what she wanted, he released her and moved down her body. He turned her so her legs were hanging off the cushions. Spreading them, he crawled in close while sliding her jeans and panties down to her knees. Using his tongue, he parted her folds and found her clit. He feasted on her, flicking, sucking, caressing.

How do I keep my word now?

He never thought a woman could taste so good. To add to his arousal, she flowed freely on his tongue, spurring him on. She braced her palm to the back of his head, pushing his tongue deeper into her. Miracle gripped his shoulders before arching and shouting his name. He felt her drip down his chin and Beast took great pleasure in that.

When he moved up her once more, Beast brought her underwear and jeans with him. Miracle had her eyes closed, her lips parted and her body shook each time he touched her. Beast licked his lips then placed her fully on the sofa. She moaned as he covered her with a blanket from the back of the couch.

CHAPTER 5

For two days Miracle didn't speak of what they'd done. She'd spread herself open to this man, had him kiss her in the most intimate place possible, and she didn't feel the least bit guilty. In fact, she couldn't wait for him to do it again.

Also in those days, Beast took it upon himself to train her. Half the time she had no idea if he was preparing her to defend herself should he not be around or the zombie apocalypse.

"When you hit, you want to do as much damage as possible," Beast said. "You want to incapacitate your attacker so you can get away."

"I get the idea." Miracle mumbled, pulling her sore body off the mat.

"Again."

"Beast, I'm not a soldier!" Miracle snapped. "My body isn't used to this and I'm in pain! Okay? If the kidnappers come, let them because I can't do this anymore."

She turned and began storming away but Beast caught her arm and pulled her into his chest. He caressed her back, kissed her head and murmured something in French.

"I just want you to be safe, *Fleur.*"

"I get it. But I'm tired—Beast. I'm just so tired."

He stopped the drills and Miracle found her body relaxing. She worked beside him, researching her paper while working on figuring out the real identity of this man who seemed to have weirdos killing for him. On the third day, a beautiful African American woman dressed in all black let herself into the apartment.

"Hello," the newcomer said.

Miracle blinked at her, surprised.

"You remember Sabine," Beast said.

"They call me Barbie." Sabine grinned widely. "I'm the pretty one of the bunch."

It was like meeting Sabine all over again. Miracle liked her instantly—well after she realized Beast and this Aphrodite weren't an item. Turned out, Barbie wasn't just a regular cop as Miracle had thought. In fact, she was a part of Beast's team and was just like one of the guys. She had that ready smirk, that look that said she was up to something and it was going to be epic. Tex had that look, so had her brother and Beast. Soon they were joined by Zero, Mouth, and a new guy she'd never seen before called Pitbull. After twenty minutes, Miracle had laughed more than she had all year.

Mouth was aptly named. He was a fast talking, bullshit spewing loveable, African American hottie. Pitbull was quiet, the one who seemed to always be planning something. He was contemplative yet had some pretty sweet one line zingers. Zero, Japanese descent, was always blushing over something Mouth came up with. Miracle adored Zero. Then there was Barbie who seemed to be the one keeping this rag-tag bunch from becoming cavemen.

In that time the group swore Miracle to secrecy then told her they were a specialised team called CIRO that was a part of the *Grenzschutzgruppe* 9.

"Um...what?" Miracle asked.

"Short version, GSG 9," Barbie explained. "Why the hell do you have to make things so complicated, huh, Pitbull?"

The large man crinkled his nose at her and Miracle smiled. The one they called Pitbull was a big guy, muscular and she remembered wondering where he found clothes for all that bulk."What does CIRO mean?" Miracle shoved a piece of ham into her mouth.

"Central Intelligence Recon Operators." Mouth told her. "We're smaller and do mostly reconnaissance."

"Don't let that make you nervous," Zero said. "We are quite deadly. We train with the rest of the GSG 9."

"I'm not worried." Miracle was surprised at how truthful that was. "Tex trusts you. And his trust is never misplaced."

"He is kinda cool, isn't he?" Barbie giggled.

"Oh boy." The males of the group groaned in unison.

But soon, the mirth was over and they got down to business. They included her in everything, which surprised her but she wasn't going to complain.

"We don't know if he's still alive," Miracle explained. "So far, Tex and I haven't been able to find him or anyone who will claim to even know the guy. So, right now, we're, as you say, flying blind.

What little information we have may not even be accurate."

"I don't like it," Pitbull said, letting his weight fall into the sofa. The piece of furniture complained under his massive framed.

"Me either," Beast said. "Mouth, what did you find out from our friend?"

"He says some guy called him up and gave him this job," Mouth said. "He sells his services to the highest bidder. We gave Tex access to the phone, hoping he'll be able to get something off it. We also handed the suspect over to the rest of the GSG 9. If you're right, Miracle, then he can help us catch a war criminal."

"That's well and good, but I don't want to die because of this," Miracle said, a little more irritated than she probably should.

"You're not going to die," Barbie assured her. "We won't let that happen."

"I really did dig into something I shouldn't have," Miracle said.

"It's not that you shouldn't have. Sooner or later these assholes were going to go after someone," Beast explained. "It just so happened to be you."

"This is ridiculous!" Miracle frowned.

"I agree," Barbie said. "But, the horse is already

out of the barn. We now justhave to round the sucker up. Let's just pray Tex found something on that phone thatto point us in the right direction. In the mean time, we're going to need copies of all your research that has anything to do with this guy."

Miracle quickly saved a copy of her research onto a USB stick and handed it to Barbie.

"Okay. I'll get this to Tex," Barbie said.

"I thought you would go through it," Miracle said.

"No honey. I don't do the computer stuff. I'm better with a sniper rifle." Barbie rose and grabbed her coat and keys. "We should go."

"Yeah." Pitbull stood. "We have patrol."

"If you need me," Beast said. "You call."

"Ten four, boss." Mouth gave Beast a mock salute. "It'll be okay, Miracle. We're going to end this."

Miracle smiled at him and accepted a quick hug. "Thank you. I didn't mean to interrupt your lives like this."

"Lives?" Barbie chimed in. "Mouth? All you're doing is being his perfect form of contraceptive."

"Eww." Miracle made a face but chuckled. "Thanks for that."

"You're welcome!" Barbie beamed.

Mouth groaned.

"Okay, children." Beast laughed. "Out."

It took another few minutes for the guys to get out the door. Miracle laughed and shook her head after they left. Suddenly the silence was too much, so she had to do something or she'd go crazy. Instead of sitting around, she headed into the kitchen. She began washing up the dishes the team had used. The walls closed in and she suddenly realized how serious this whole situation had become. From almost being run of the road to an almost kidnapping—all of it was real.

All the time she imagined how scared Liane had been. They'd packed her up and shipped her off to Norfolk to hang out with the rest of Tex's team. Apparently she was staying with their team member, Mozart. Miracle hadn't met him yet but he was a friend of Tex's—she would trust him.

"*Fleur*?"

"I can't talk right now. I'm busy."

"Miracle, stop."

But she merely kept scrubbing the plate she had in her hand. Beast reached around her and took it away, turned off the water and removed the washcloth from her fingers. He then took her shoulders and turned her to him. When they faced each other,

Beast took her lips like soldiers storming a beach. Miracle moaned, gripped his hips and melted into his chest. Kissing him again sent the same electricity to jolt through her as before. All the worries she had before, the fear, the anxiety vanished.

But the kiss didn't last nearly as long as Miracle wanted it to.

"What was—what was that—for?" Miracle panted, her eyes still closed.

"I need you to relax," Beast said.

"So you kiss me?" Miracle glared at him. "That did nothing to make me calm. It just turned me on!"

He smiled.

Miracle stepped from his arms and stormed from the room. The heavy fall of his footsteps followed her out the room until he caught her and trapped her against a wall in the corridor toward the bedroom.

"I made you wet, Miracle?" Beast asked, dragging a large palm up her thigh. He pushed her hips into the surface of the wall before grinding his hardness into her. "That makes me very happy."

"But you promised. No sex until afterward."

"I know." Beast bowed his head to nip at her shoulder. "I remember. I hate that I made that deal, but I did. In the meantime, let me make you feel good, take your mind off what's happening for a little while."

Miracle blinked at him.

"All you have to do is say no..."

"I don't want to say no." Miracle lifted her chin. "I *really* don't want to say no."

"Good."

Miracle wasn't sure what to expect but she wanted this. She searched her heart for an hesitation, but found none.

Slowly, Beast stripped her naked then stood with his back against the opposite wall to stare at her. The action was so invading, so personal, so overly intimate, her cheeks burned. When she moved her hand to cover her breasts, one look from Beast had here dropping her arms back to her sides. She'd always been critical of her weight, that her body wasn't perfect. Standing the way she was, with Beast silent and staring sent fear mixed with arousal coursing through her veins

"What are you doing?" Miracle asked.

"Watching you bloom," Beast said.

Miracle bowed her head as her cheeks flared fire. Even though she had her head down, somehow she knew precisely where he was looking. Heat followed his stare up her thighs, across her hips then up her stomach. When his gaze reached her breasts, Miracle had to look at him. He was chewing on his bottom lip but his eyes dawdled for a mere minute before it was on the move again.

"Turn around," Beast said. "Arch your back."

With a soft sigh, she turned and pressed her breasts into the wall. When she glanced over her shoulder, Beast was walking toward her. He pressed a hand to the center of her back while the other stroke over the curve of her ass. He tapped one cheek, then the other, making Miracle sigh.

"Every part of you excites me." Beast said in her ear. "The way you tremble in my arms, the sound of your breath quickening, feeling your skin pepper with goose-bumps—and knowing all of this is because of me."

His words floated around her brain, pushing her closer to an orgasm. This was akin to phone sex, listening to the naughty words of the other and getting off on the power of them. Only, Beast was with her and he had his wonderful hands all over her body. One hand making her moan the other, tweaking hr nipples. Miracle moaned and allowed her head to fall to the side and he took that as an invitation to nibble at her neck.

"Say my name," Beast demanded.

"Beast..."

"My name, *Fleur*."

He dragged large finger over her clit and she had no choice.

"Alric!"

CHAPTER 6

Beast didn't like leaving Miracle on her own. He'd spent the whole time, after CIRO was called in for a mission, trying to convince himself not wanting to leave her was only because of his growing feelings for her. After all, his building was pretty secure. And it wasn't like he was off gallivanting around the place.

Duty called.

His commanding officer had agreed to send a patrol to sit on the place but Beast was still uncomfortable with it. No one could protect her like he could. He checked over his G3K rifle and set it on the large table in the room as his team milled around preparing their weapons. He inhaled, held the breath, trying to switch his mind from Miracle tot he mission at hand.

If he couldn't focus, one or more of his guys would not make it home.

"All right," Beast said after clearing his throat. "We move out in ten."

"Sir!" They acknowledged him.

Mouth, Zero, and Pitbull left the room but he could feel Barbie hovering. He smiled and faced her already knowing what she wanted to talk about.

"Okay. I was wondering when you'd get around to it." Beast lifted a booted foot to a chair to fix his lace. "What's on your mind?"

"You and Miracle..."

"Yeah?"

"You are serious, right? This is not a game for you."

"Why are you asking?"

"Because she's a nice girl," Barbie said. "I know how you cats operate."

Beast drew the laces in tight and tied them. He lowered his foot to the floor and faced her. "You think I'm in this to hurt her?"

"Are you?"

"No! Of course not." Beast rubbed the back of his neck. "But I'm not going to lie. I don't know what *this* is. All I know is I feel something for her and I want to see where it goes. I don't even know if she feels it too."

"Have you slept together?"

"No." He reached for his rifle. "It's not like we don't want to—but I didn't feel right sleeping with her with danger lurking. I mean, if we were to sleep together I want it to be because she wants to and not because she sees me as some kind of savior."

"Now, that's a load of crap." Barbie picked up the Steyr AUG A3 rifle and raised a brow at him. "Sex is sex. It becomes more if you feel something else for the other person. I see it in your eyes, Beast—you want more."

Beast groaned. "It doesn't matter what I want or what I feel if the feelings aren't mutual. No means no."

"Has she said no to you?"

"No."

"Then?"

Beast shook his head and shrugged.

"Oh, I see—when it comes to work you're beast mode—all the time. But a little feelings and you go chicken?"

"I haven't—can we get this mission over with? I really want to go back to her."

"She'll be fine."

"Yeah, and then she's going to leave..."

Barbie tilted her head. "As in go back home? Well, yeah, that's a strong possibility. You just have to give her a reason to stay."

But Beast said nothing. Instead he exited the room and joined up with the gathering outside. Barbie wasn't far behind and they piled into the transport. As usual the drive to the drop was silent. No one said anything and half the time Beast wondered if they were all breathing. Still, he remained quiet, head down, and put Miracle and her flawless perfection to the back of his head.

The first drop was Barbie so she could set up to cover them if they needed it. At the main stop, Zero and Mouth alighted first followed by Beast and Pitbull. Afterward, a scurry of activities carried them into the two story building. Every movement was quick, precise.

"Barbie." Beast called after clearing yet another room. "Report."

"Clear." Barbie's voice was crisp through the earpiece.

The team finally converged on the final door. When Mouth tested it, the knob didn't budge and they couldn't play around with it. Any noise would alert whoever inside of their presence and the hostages would be dead. Beast knew they would have to go in loud which meant once the door came down, they were going to have to go in hard.

Pitbull looked toward him and Beast nodded. He backed up with the others and Pitbull stepped forward. He placed a black disc against the back of the door. As he stepped away, Beast palmed a flash-bang. After the disc beeped once, there was a loud bang and the door fell forward. Beast and Zero hurled flashbangs into the room then charged in first.

"GSG 9!" Beast shouted.

That must have been the wrong thing to say for all hell broke loose. He quickly located the hostages and moved wide away from them to draw fire at himself. He fired, taking out one kidnapper while Zero handled another. There was a slurping sound and Beast glanced behind him to see a man almost as if he was frozen in time with a hole through the side of his head.

Barbie struck again.

By the time the smoke cleared and they evacuated all the hostages, Beast was exhausted. He went back to base with his team. It took some time to debrief them and to complete all the reports necessary before any of them could leave. Exhausted, he climbed onto his motorcycle and headed straight to his apartment.

The moment he pulled into the parking lot he knew something wasn't right. The squad car sent to watch over Miracle sat with all its doors opened. On the passenger side, the officer was hanging out, throat slit. On the driver's side the cop had a bullet to the chest.

Beast parked the cycle and charged into the building. As he moved, he called in the officers down, and then dropped his phone into his pocket. By the time he made it to his unit, his exhaustion had long since been forgotten. When he entered and found the place ransacked, the fear quickly morphed to rage.

"*Fleur*?" He called going from through the place. "Miracle?"

When he confirmed she wasn't there, he sent a text to his team with one simple word. "SOS."

He then called Tex.

"Beast—what's the word?" Tex answered.

"I fucked up" Beast paced one way then the other. He dragged his free palm over his head. "I fucked up and now she's gone."

"Beast—calm down. Tell me what's goin' on,

brother."

"We had a mission. I don't even know why we were called. GSG 9/1 was available. Anyway, we had to leave her. The commander sent a squad car to keep watch, but now I'm back, they're dead and she's gone! Tex, find her!"

"Okay, I'll do my best. In the mean time what's your plan?"

"I'm waiting for the rest of the guys to show up. Once they're here, we can start digging."

"Good. I'll send Dude your way as well." Tex promised. "Turn on your computer. I need to send you what I found. Maybe it will help us narrow down where she is."

Beast hurried to do what Tex asked. "Done."

"She figured out who Heinrik was." Tex's voice was hard.

"She didn't tell me."

"Well, I don't think she knew she figured it out," Tex said. "I had to have the picture restored to get a face. My guess is, whoever this guy is now, thinks she knows more than she does and he wants to get the proof back and shut her up. She'll be fine if she doesn't say anything."

Oh God.

"Tex, please..."

"Hang tight, brother. I'll hit you back," Tex said and was gone.

Though he was tempted to hurl the phone across the room, Beast set it on the table beside the laptop instead. He watched as the screen to his computer came alive and files began opening.

Tex at work.

He paced a path into the floor waiting for the rest of CIRO to show up. He then busied himself going through the files and photos Tex had sent. When they were all there, including Dude, Beast faced them.

"Where's Miracle?" Faulker "Dude" Cooper asked.

"They took her while we were on a mission," Beast said. "Now, I have to get her back."

"What's this *I* business?" Barbie asked. "Like you always say, Beast, there's no I in the word team."

"This mission will not be sanctioned." Beast told her. "You know that."

"And your point is?" Dude asked.

"We're not going anywhere," Zero said. "Your woman is missing and none of us are going home until she's back."

"She's not my—" Beast started.

"Deny it all you want." Mouth peeled off his

leather jacket and tossed it over the back of a chair. "But we all know better. Now, what did Tex send you?"

"Let's recap what we know." Beast swallowed convulsively then picked up the laptop. "Miracle was digging into a man name Heinrik Loft. He was about fourteen years old at the end of World War 2. He was kind of an adopted son to Hitler. When Miracle started digging, someone tried running her off the road and a couple of days ago they tried grabbing her at the mall. Now, for the new bits. Tex did some nosing around and found Heinrik Loft."

"He's still alive?" Barbie asked.

Beast handed her a picture. She looked at it and gasped.

"Yes. And he's..." Beast swallowed. The anger pulsed inside him like a simmering volcano.

"No way," Mouth murmured looking at the image over Barbie's shoulder before she passed it to Zero.

"Who is he?" Dude asked.

"Take a closer look," Zero handed the picture to Dude.

"*Oberstleutnant* Hunfried?" Dude asked.

"He is a cop! How could he be the same guy?" Mouth asked. "There has to be an explanation."

It all makes sense then—why Hunfried had sent CIRO to the hostage situation. He wanted to get them away from Miracle.

"Like I said." Beast growled. "Anyone who wants to back out, now is the time."

"Lay off the bullshit, would you?" Dude snapped. "You're a part of this family and if one of us is hurting then all of us are hurting."

"What's the plan?" Barbie asked.

"We find Miracle." Beast snarled. "We go through every single level of Hunfried's life if we have to. We get Miracle back. Then we burn his world to the ground."

CHAPTER 7

Before Miracle even opened her eyes, pain throbbed through her. Moving her leg was a bad idea. Each inch she pulled it up, Miracle's body throbbed as though she'd been hit by a car. It took a few more seconds for her to remember where she was and what had happened. They wanted a picture—and she had no idea what they were talking about. Throughout her research on Heinrik she had yet to find one usable picture of the kid.

"Think happy thoughts." Miracle managed through gritted teeth. "Think happy thoughts. Be positive. You have SEALs and GSG 9-CIRO on your side. Walls mean nothing to them and Tex can find anything and anyone. Everything will work out."

Her little pep talk didn't work. Tears still stung her eyes threatening to fall.

"Who am I kidding? I don't even know where the hell I am."

Miracle sighed and shifted again, biting into her sore bottom lip against the pain. She closed her eyes again, deciding to try a new tactic.

"There's no place like home. There's no place like home." She muttered. After a pause, Miracle opened one eye to look around.

Nope—still in hell.

Well, you can't believe everything you read.

After all she'd been through in the last couple of weeks, Miracle was willing to go on a little faith—even if it was blind, deaf and dumb faith.

After they'd taken her from Beast's place, they'd worked her over. But she couldn't tell them what she didn't know. Grunting, she wrapped her right arm against her left side and pushed into sitting position.

The room was dark and smelled like mold and cat pee. Remembering what her brother had taught her, she closed her eyes for a moment and listened. There had to be something to give her an idea of where she was. Then again, she didn't get out much since arriving in Germany. It had all been about the library and interviews, digging through dusty, old books and archives.

She gave up on that and instantly her mind went to wondering if Beast was looking for her. The thought of his name brought her back to him, the way he smelled, the size of his body, the heat to fill his eyes when he looked at her. How did it all come to this?

All Miracle wanted was to pass her dissertation. She wanted to make something of herself rather than sit around and live off the blood money in her bank account.

It wass what it was, right?

Blood money?

Her parents had to both die for her to get it. After she got her credentials, she could have become a teacher and work a little money for herself—make her own way. Creating her own fortune had been important to her. Instead she was stuck in a situation that could get both her and the people she cared for killed.

The sound of a lock being thrown drew her from her thoughts and she eased back into the wall. A large man entered and grabbed her by the hair. He hauled her from the room and Miracle didn't resist, gritting her teeth against the pain. He tossed her into the center of a room where she skidded across the damp, rough floor. She crashed into the wall hard, grunting as the movements jarred her ribs.

Yup. I'm pretty sure one or more of these are cracked.

A beat of water hit her in the face. Her first instinct was to inhale and since she couldn't stop her body from listening, Miracle turned her face away. The water hit her neck hard, forcing her into the hard surface behind her as a voice barked orders through a speaker.

"Where is the picture?" He demanded. "You can save yourself a lot of pain if you tell me."

Miracle coughed and sputtered but remained quiet. There were only so many times she could say something before giving up. She wasn't sure how long the torture continued before they stopped and the large man dragged her back to her prison and hurled her in. Before he tossed her, she pulled his cell phone from his pocket and shoved it down her shirt. As she fell, Miracle twisted her body so she would fall against her back.

Though she protected the phone and her ribs, all she could do was curl soundlessly on the floor, her eyes wide. It hurt so bad she couldn't even scream. She allowed her body to calm down before she pulled the cell out and activated the screen. It wasn't password protected which was strange but good for her. The first thing she did was ensure it was on silence. It ringing as she was trying to hide it wouldn't have been a good thing. She tried remembering Beast's number but she hadn't bother getting used to the numbers. So, Miracle did the only thing she could. She tried calling Tex but couldn't get through. She gritted her teeth and eased to her feet and moved close to the grilled window. She texted him instead.

Tex it's Mira...

Miracle thought better and deleted it. Just in case the text was intercepted, using her name was a bad idea. Instead, she sent a simple text.

Fleur. SOS.

After ten minutes, no reply.

Fleur. SOS.

Another fifteen minutes past and she was about to send another message when the phone vibrated in her palm. She glanced down at the screen to see a text message from a blocked number.

Texas is listening.

Miracle wanted to cheer then. She wanted to do back-flips but refrained from both. There was a sound on the other side of the door so she reached up, through the grills and set the phone, on the ledge outside. Hopefully it didn't rain or the battery didn't die. Tex wouldn't be able to track it if either of those things happened.

The moment she was sitting on the floor again, the door opened and a different man grabbed her.

Beast got it.

Now he knew how Tex felt when Melody was in danger. The helplessness, the sadness, the absolute rage to surge through him was indescribable. Sure, they hadn't declared their intentions ot feelings for one another. It had been too soon but Beast should have known better. In his line of work, he should've known regular timing meant nothing. Tomorrow was never promised, especially when someone carried a gun for a living. So, when someone like Miracle entered his life—he should've embraced it. He should've made love to her when he had the chance, held her all night, felt her heart beat against him.

Those were all regrets—and he swore a long time ago he'd never have any.

"Where are you *ma petit Fleur*?" Beast whispered. "Why can't I find you?"

He gripped the railing. Hunfried had suddenly

disappeared. Which meant Beast was in charge of CIRO until he could be found—

And I put a bullet between his eyes.

But the man was nowhere to be found. No one in his family knew where he'd gone off to but they didn't seem worried. Honestly, Beast didn't think they cared if he was alive or had fallen off the edge of the earth.

When it came to Hunfried's friends, CIRO had tried being discreet but after asking nicely and not getting any results, Barbie suggested knocking in some heads. Beast was more than happy with the idea. Brute force wasn't always the answer, but to find Miracle and bring her home alive, he wasn't above stooping to that level.

After having to use his fists a few times, they received more information. Now, Tex was busy digging through it all. In the mean time, CIRO was sitting around at GSG 9 headquarters, twiddling their damn thumbs.

"We *are* going to find her." Mouth's voice was soft behind him. "We've never left a man behind yet and we're not about to start now."

Beast turned and patted his friend's shoulder. "All my life, they've told me when you care for someone and that person is in danger, you should be able to feel it—to feel the person. Why can't I feel her? Don't I care enough?"

"No." Mouth stood beside him. "Don't ever do that. There is no magic to any of this. You're not telepathic and there's no such thing as telekinesis. And because there is no such thing, you have us. And we're fantastic at what we do. Now, let's—"

"Beast!" Pitbull came running out onto the balcony.

Beast swirled around. He couldn't remember ever seeing Pitbull so animated—so excited. "What's up?"

"Do you know someone by the name of, Floor?" Pitbull asked.

"What?" Mouth and Beast chorused.

"That's what Tex said. Floor." Pitbull glanced down at the piece of paper.

"Lemme see." Beast took it and looked down.

Fleur.

"You mean, Fleur!" Beast exclaimed. "Fleur, Pit. It's French for flower. It's what I call Miracle."

"You two have nicknames now?" Pitbull quirked a brow.

"We'll talk about it later." Beast barged inside to find Barbie still on the line with Tex. He took the phone from her. "Tex."

"Yeah, brother?"

"How did you get this?" Beast asked.

"I got a text message saying *Fleur SOS.* I assumed it was Miracle reachin' out and tracked the cell."

"So you know where she is?"

Movement caught his attention and Beast glanced behind him to see Dude, Barbie, Mouth, Zero, and Pitbull were already suiting up.

"You underestimate me, Beast. You hurt my feelins."

Beast smiled. "You sent it to the guys?"

"Oh yeah. Now, go get your woman."

"She's not my—"

"Yeah. Yeah." Tex drawled. "We can fight about that later. I'll send the floor plans for the place. Keep in mind the floor plan is like a million years old so there could be some updates they didn't post. I'll also be on the comm."

"Heinrik, Hunfried?" Beast asked.

"Still lookin'. There's been no activities on his credit cards since yesterday and nothing on his cell phone. But there are cameras everywhere. I'll find him."

Beast hung up and grabbed his vest. Once he was strapped in, he shoved his Glock into the holster on his hip and all of them piled out for the transport.

Zero took over for the regular driver while Pitbull slid underneath the truck to remove the tracking device. Hunfield was the ringleader of all of this and Beast didn't know who else within the ranks was involved in the cover-up. If CIRO couldn't be tracked, his team would be safe.

"Okay, so this building right here is the highest point and I would have a great view of ground zero," Barbie said, tapping away at the tablet. "But I don't know how much I'll be able to cover you. According to this plan the building was built back in the war days—it's like a concrete monstrosity. Once you go in, I won't have eyes on you."

"Let me see," Dude said. "Interesting. I could set up some C4 with blasting caps here and here—wait for you guys to find Miracle, then blow it. That should give you eyes on the inside."

"Hmm." Zero mused from the driver's seat. "Good idea but we don't know if any part of it is load bearing."

"Well, I need eyes inside," Barbie said. "Like I said, this place was built during World War 2 so it's like a fucking fortress. It's either the wall goes or I go in with you."

"You're going to have to go in with us." Beast

decided. "I have a feeling we'll need all the help we can get."

"Got it," Barbie said.

"But just in case, Dude, set the explosives."

"There should be some in that kit under the seat." Pitbull pointed out.

Dude nodded.

"We can enter through here," Beast said, taping his tablet. He knew whatever he touched would light up on the other team members' tablets. "Dude, you and Barbie head to the wall. Zero and I will take lead. Mouth, you and Pitbull will get our six. Whoever finds Miracle first, radios in a location and heads to the nearest exit with her. Now, this is going to be hard since we don't know what room she's in, so we can't set an extraction point. If we don't find her, we exit here. And we meet back where we park. Any questions?"

"By the way," Dude said. "I'm not supposed to be heading out on ops while I'm here..."

"Ops?" Pitbull asked. "What Op?"

The others laughed.

"We're not trying to start an international incident," Mouth said. "Trust me. You're not here."

Beast exhaled and checked the time. They were six minutes out."

“Six minutes,” Zero called from the front seat. “We go in on foot from Aaubast. We can use the trees to hide the truck from the road.”

“Roger that.” Beast agreed. Reaching into his pocket, he pulled out an earpiece and stuck it into his right ear. He squeezed the back of it. “Tex.”

“At your service, brother,” the comforting voice of the computer genius said.

CHAPTER 8

"For the last time," Miracle said, her body numb, her teeth chattering. She'd been dunked under frigid cold water so many times, she'd lost track. "I don't—know where it is. All I have—is a name."

"No one is coming to save you," the man torturing her said in really bad English. "If that's why you're holding out. We have all the time in the world for you to tell us what we want to hear."

That's what you think—the Beast is coming...

"I don't know what you're talking about." Miracle caught her breath as best she could. "I don't care about any picture. I just wanted research for my dissertation."

She was rewarded with another submersion into the tank. After so many times, she stopped struggling. The water stung the cuts and buries on her body and face. The air evaporated faster than it had before and she inhaled because her brain didn't know better. Coughing under water, puttering, feeling the ice cold liquid seep into her lungs, Miracle knew she was going to die. Beast and Tex didn't know where she was and she didn't make love to Beast or have the chance to see if they could build something worthwhile together. And she was going to die without ever knowing what it felt like to be loved.

Her captor yanked her above water again and her hungry lungs clamored for air. She coughed, sputtered. Her throat burned, her eyes ached and her body trembled.

Still they asked for the picture. If she knew where it was, Miracle would have told them if only to stop the torture. But she didn't. Even though she knew they wouldn't let her go.

And somewhere in the background, Miracle's frazzled brain could have sworn someone was playing *Raindrops Keep Falling on my Head.* The first time they dunked her, they'd been playing a song by the Beach Boys.

If I ever make it out of this, anyone who even mentions those songs will be getting a foot up their ass.

From somewhere in the bleakness of her mind, she remembered Beast's training. But she could barely lift her hand much less attack anyone. Her captor seemed to have gotten tired because he ordered her be brought back to her cell. She was tossed in and crashed into the wall. Miracle felt nothing. After her body thawed, she'd be bruised and battered all over..

There was no getting out. The place was like a prison—no windows she'd seen except the grilled one in her cell. It was barely big enough to get her head out. She remembered two doors—one was boarded up and the other was heavily guarded. Even if she did manage to step out the door, she wouldn't get very far before she'd be dead.

Exhausted, Miracle barely had enough strength to roll to her back. The minutes ticked by and her body began feeling a bit better. They hadn't fed her and Miracle was starving.

No, screw that.

"I'm not going to die here," Miracle murmured. "I might get killed but it won't be in this filthy hovel." She gritted her teeth, held her breath and pushed her wet, matted hair from her face. Bracing her free hand on the floor, she dragged herself to the wall closer to the door. "I'm not going to die here. Not like this—not before..."

She looked up at the single light bulb in the ceiling then out the window. It had gotten dark.

I'm not going to die here became her mantra as she sucked in the pain to rise to her feet. She stuck her hand out the window, feeling for the cell phone. Her fingers knocked into it and it almost fell to the ground before she could grab it. She sighed in relief and checked the screen. She had two bars of power left.

Calling Texas. She tried sending but apparently the network was down. Miracle sighed as another idea flashed through her mind. She shuffled over to the door and pressed her ear to it. When nothing caught her attention, she wrapped her shirt around her fist and stood underneath the light bulb. She knew stretching her arms above her head would hurt like hell but it had to be done. Holding her breath, she pushed to her tiptoes and stretched for the bulb. Thankfully, the ceiling was low enough and she was able to loosen the bulb. With that done, Miracle slipped back into her shirt, picked up the cell and waited.

This may be the dumbest idea in the history of dumb ideas or she was a genius. Whatever happened, she was ready to end this. Miracle exhaled carefully before inching to a spot behind the door.

She didn't have to wait long. Soon, the lock on the door fell loose and a frame moved into the doorway and reached for the light switch. He flicked it and when nothing happened, he moved into the room and turned his back to her. Like Beast had taught her, she snuck up behind him and with the cell phone gripped in a tight fist, she bashed him against the side of the head with all the power she could muster. He howled in pain but she merely pushed the door closed as he hit the ground. Without wasting time, Miracle dove on him. Repeatedly, she brought the phone down until it shattered and he went limp.

That's gonna smart in the morning.

She used his own shirt to gag him then tied his arms behind his back before grabbing what she could off him. The gun she hid in the same place she had her phone. It wouldn't do her any good since she wouldn't know what to do with the damn thing. She'd only fired a gun once—Curtis had taken her to a private range. After one squeeze of the trigger, she'd given up and handed the weapon back to him.

She shrugged and stuck her head out the door

and glanced both ways up and down the corridor. Since she'd been blindfolded when they brought her in, she didn't know which way was out. But Tex had replied. He had to know where she was and all she had to do was stay away from the bad guys.

The clock was ticking. There was no time to sit and pussyfoot around. It was either left or right and live—or die. Exhaling, a surge of adrenaline filled her and she went left.

But Miracle quickly became lost and walked right back into the arms of her captors.

The sun was gone and CIRO along with Dude, moved under the cover of Darkness. They made entry silently and instantly Dude and Barbie veered off to their positions. Beast continued with rest of his team, clearing one room after another. From what he remembered of the schematics, there was a basement, but the upper floor had too many spaces to go through. Beast found himself slowly losing his patience. Deep down he knew impatience could lead to one of his team members getting shot. Mistakes happened the team leader's mind isn't in on the mission. He had to focus. Instead of letting it consume him, he inhaled slowly, held it, then exhaled.

"We're in position." Dude's voice rang through his headpiece in his left ear. "We have the wake-up call set?"

"I found a perch." Barbie announced soon after.

"Roger." Beast acknowledged.

As they rounded a corner, they came in contact with their first two assailants.

"GSG 9!" Beast shouted. "*Legen sie ihre waffe nach unten*!"

"Weapons down!" Pitbull shouted in English in case.

But these men weren't listening. Instead, they advanced with their guns up. Beast lost his patience and shot one between the eyes.Zero got the other in the chest. Mouth ensured they were dead and the group continued on their way, faster now. They were sure someone heard the shots and soon they'd be in the thick of everything.

"We have contact." Beast spoke into his communicator. "I repeat. We have contact. Watch your six."

"Roger." Dude said.

"I got him," Barbie said.

They came to a final door, and when Zero tested it, the handle wouldn't budge. From the other side of it was the sound of water splashing and screaming. Beast's ire rose to the boiling point. He twisted to look at Pitbull who understood what he wanted without a word passing between them.

Pitbull stepped forward, attached a black, rounded disk to the door close to the handle. Beast and the others backed up as the disc beeped once then exploded. The smoke quickly evaporated and the four of them charged into the room. The room was empty except for a tank in the center. A man stood, back to the group leaning over the side as water splashed everywhere.

"GSG 9!" Mouth hollered.

The man stopped and pulled a figure from the tank. Miracle came into view, but Beast didn't have time to feel much of anything because she was quickly yanked in front of the man who used to be his boss. Beast wanted to run to her, to pull her into his arms to make sure she was safe. He wanted to apologise for taking his eyes off her and to promise he would never do it again if she stayed with him.

"Tex, we found her," Beast said.

"Is she okay?" Tex asked.

"Not yet—I'll have to call you back."

"Beast don't—"

But Beast removed the earpiece and dropped it

into his pocket.

Please—Beast pleaded internally. *Hold on.*

Loft now had a gun to Miracle's temple and Beast couldn't believe how blinding the urge to shoot the idiot in the head was to him.

"Let her go, Loft." Zero demanded. "You're not getting out of here."

"Okay." Loft began backing away from the tank and further into the room. "Neither is she."

Beast growled.

"Easy, brother." Mouth warned.

Beast frowned. He released his rifle and let it fall against his body but pulled out his Glock 17 and trained it at the man.

"What are you doing?" Pitbull asked.

"Drop—your—weapon." Beast warned. He inched forward.

"Beast?" Miracle asked, her voice weak.

"I'm here, *Fleur.*"

"Stay back!" Loft demanded. "I'm your superior here! I order you to stand down."

"We're through taking orders from you." Pitbull's voice held ice.

" I'm not going to jail!" Loft sounded unhinged. "I won't spend the rest of my life in some cell like an animal."

"Funny," Mouth said out loud. "He thinks prison is where we want him to go at this point."

"Trust me, Loft," Beast said. "We're *way* past the arresting phase."

"What're you going to do? Kill me?" Loft scoffed. "I'm a cop! You'd burn. And besides, anything happens to me and she gets a bullet."

Anger surged through Beast. He was finished trying to reason with this fool. Though, if it was up to him he'd drop the asshole like a sack of potatoes and not think twice about it. But Miracle was there and even though Beast knew he wouldn't miss his target, she'd gone through enough.

Still, Beast was done playing good cop or even a halfway decent cop. He reached up and removed his helmet then facemask. He dropped them to the floor.

"Beast," Zero said, concern filling his voice.

"This is going to end now," Beast replied. "One final time, Loft. Let's make this all official. I am Alric, Beastmode, Gerhart, Commanding Officer of the GSG 9 CIRO. You are under arrest for crimes against humanity, two counts of murder, and the kidnapping and torture of a civilian. You *will* drop your weapon and come peacefully or you *will* die."

"I want a car outside, gassed up..." Loft began.

"Miracle, whatever you do," Beast said as if Loft hadn't spoken. "Don't move. Keep very still."

"You're not listening!" Loft shrieked. "I'll kill her, I swear to God!"

"To God?" Pitbull asked. "Seriously?"

"The only thing you're getting is a one way ticket to the Haque," Beast said. "Or a bullet. What is your decision?"

Beast received his answer by the change in Loft's body, the slight rise of his shoulder, the twitch in his eye. Inhaling, Beast squeezed his trigger and within seconds, one of his bullets lodged itself in Loft's right eye. The boom caused Miracle to scream but as he'd instructed, she remained perfectly still.

Maybe it was fear from him discharging a weapon so close to her.

She closed her eyes as Loft's arm fell from her throat and he slipped to the floor. The gun he'd held to her head clattered to the side and while Zero and Mouth ensured the room was secure, Pitbull hurried over and kicked Loft's gun away.

Beast rushed to Miracle and caught her against his chest before she hit the floor. The others were busy talking into their comm units

"Darling, I'm so sorry." Beast whispered, pushing

matted hair from her face. "Please tell me you're okay."

"What—what took you so long?" Miracle panted. A small smile graced her lips.

"I'm sorry, *ma petit Fleur*." Beast bowed his head and brushed his lips to her forehead. "I'll never let you down again."

She smiled bigger up at him and closed her eyes. His heart lurched as panic filled him.

"Baby? I need you to stay awake, okay?" Beast asked. "Open your eyes."

She did. "I'm so tired."

"I know, *Fleur*, but stay awake."

"Beast?" Pitbull said.

"Yeah?" Beast glanced over at him.

"He's dead and we have a clean-up crew on the way." Pitbull announced.

"Room's clear," Mouth said.

"Good," Beast said, scooping Miracle into his arms. "Get the others to meet us at the extraction point. I need to get her some air."

Finally outside, Beast sat on the ground with Miracle cuddled to his chest. He made eye contact with her and smiled while using a finger to push some hair off her cheek. "I shouldn't have left you."

He told her. "I knew he was out there. I shouldn't have left you. I'm so sorry."

"Alric—you *will* stop apologizing. I'm going to be okay."

He nodded but he couldn't help the culpability raging through him like a tornado.

"You'll have to take me on a date," Miracle said.

"What?"

"A date. You know, when two people, who kinda like each other, go out on the town—together—alone?"

Beast laughed. "I know what a date is, *Fleur.* And you kinda like me? I don't know if *kinda* is enough."

"You're cute and all, but I have to make sure you're a gentleman and that my father would approve."

"Your father..."

"Died a few years ago. But I know the kind of man he'd want for me."

"I'm sorry for your loss."

She exhaled loudly. "Thank you. So—the date?"

"You have a deal." Beast promised. "It would be an honor."

"Then I have to go shopping..."

Beast knew why she kept talking. It was her way of staying awake like he'd asked. He didn't care the reason—he just wanted her to be okay. Happily, he talked, flirted, and brushed soft kisses across her forehead. The cleanup crew were still a little way out. Beast was about to say something else to her when he remembered Tex was still waiting.

He pulled the earpiece out of his pocket, where he'd stashed it, and stuck it in his ear. He activated it. Tex's worried voice filled his head.

"I have her in my arms," Beast said. "She's okay."

"Good. I assume you're going' to want some private time with her before I speak with her?" Tex asked.

"You would assume right." Beast's voice cracked. "You're not upset, are you?"

"Upset?" Tex asked. "Why do you ask?"

"Her and I—getting um, close. I know you heard all that."

Tex laughed. "I've known her a while and she's been looking for a good man. I'm not her father, Beast. I'm her brother."

"And sometimes brothers are the ones who are most dangerous."

Tex laughed. "You'd be right with that one. All I want is for her to be happy."

"I can do that..."

"All right. I've sent all the incriminating information to the GSG 9. So you shouldn't have any trouble when they arrive. Only—can you have Dude out of there before..."

"Right! I forgot." Beast looked up to where Dude was hanging with the rest of his team. "Dude," Beast called. "Get out of here. Wait for us at the transport."

Dude jogged over and hunched down beside them. "Hello, beautiful," Dude said. "Curtis would've haunted my ass if anything had happened to you."

"Really? I don't think so. He didn't even like me." Miracle joked.

Dude, laughed and kissed her head.

"And Cheyenne would have my head if anything happened to you." Miracle countered.

"We'll talk later. Right now I have to make myself scarce. Technically, I'm not here." Dude winked at her.

"Okay. I'll see you soon."

Dude patted Beast's shoulder and took off at a steady jog back through the wooded area and toward where they'd hidden their ride. The rest of CIRO approached them and leaned in to speak to Miracle. Each touched her cheek gently as they murmured words of happiness for her safety. When they were all through, Beast pulled her tighter into his chest, rested his head back and closed his eyes.

CHAPTER 9

Though the doctor wanted to treat Miracle privately, Beast wouldn't have it. He reluctantly left the room, but not until Miracle agreed to have Barbie remain. Barbie smiled and winked at her. Miracle relaxed on the bed while the doctor prodded and poked. He stared into her eyes, listened to her chest and her back, pressed parts of her throat. Between all this he scribbled against a chart, set it on the bed, tested her reflexes then muttered something about getting her prepped for an MRI. After more tests, he suggested a CT scan. He wanted to see if there were any issues with her brain after being on the brink of drowning so many times.

"You didn't break anything," the doctor said.

"You're going to be bruised, sore and swollen in some places for a few days. But you're a lucky woman."

Miracle felt lucky. She managed a smile.

Finally, before the doctor left the room, to set up the tests, he listened to her lungs again, scribbled in his chart and left with it.

"Is Beast always this ornery?" Miracle asked, pulling the hospital gown around her needlessly. It barely covered her ass. She didn't want to accidentally flash poor Barbie.

"Only when he cares for someone," Barbie replied. "And the short time since he's met you, you've gotten a nickname and had him go rogue. I'd say he cares."

Miracle's cheeks burned. "I care about him too." Her voice cracked with emotion. "He's different than other men, you know? And the fact that the first time I met him he was half naked and grinding on me—is only a bonus."

Barbie grinned. "Yeah. It seems I've been meeting men the wrong way."

"I'd say. You need to get with the times." Miracle laughed.

Beast entered the room then and sat on the side

of her bed. Barbie patted Miracle's shoulder and silently let. Alone with him, Miracle shifted so she could look up at him. He smiled at her then leaned in to kiss her deeply. Miracle moaned and pressed a palm to his chest.

"You scared me, *Fleur.*" Beast admitted, lifting his head to drop feather light kisses to her forehead, between her eyes, against her chin then her lips. "I was so terrified I'd never see you again."

"I wasn't worried." She lied easily. "I knew once Tex got my message, you wouldn't be far. I tried getting out and hiding but I didn't know the layout of the place and..."

"So, the man with the cloth in his mouth and the bash against the head was you?" Beast asked. "We found him in a small room."

Miracle nodded.

"That's my girl."

She grinned.

"You know the deal we made about not making love until this was all over?" Beast asked.

"Mmhmm."

"It's stupid."

"I agree."

"So." Beast smoothed a large hand down one of

her thigh then up another. "What're we going to do about it?"

Miracle toyed with the front of his shirt, watching her fingers skim over the material. "Well, when we get out of here, you'll take me home..."

"To my home."

"To your home." Miracle corrected. "And I'll take a bath. Then, I'll wait for you, naked in your bed. Is that something you could deal with?"

"I'll learn." He smirked. "But baby, you've been through hell. You're in pain. I can wait."

"I didn't break anything," Miracle said. "Ask my doctor. I'm sore, yes but I want you."

"I'll wait until tomorrow before we make love."

"Beast. I'm not fragile."

"*Fleur,* please just trust me. Once you're healed, I will do anything you want to your body."

Miracle's heart leapt with joy and nervousness. If she played her cards right, she'd be having her Beast very soon. After a few more searing kisses, the doctor cleared his throat and the reluctance in Beast's eyes caused Miracle to touch his cheek. "It's okay, hon."

"We must take *Fräulein* Jones for her scans now. Once she has completed those, she will be free to go home, if we do not find any abnormalities."

Miracle nodded.

A few female nurses entered and helped her from her bed and into a wheelchair. Though she wanted to protest, she didn't want to worry Beast any more than she already had. She blew him a kiss before they wheeled her from the room. As they made their way along the corridor, she glanced back to see Barbie walking liesurely along behind her nurses.

Miracle smiled.

After Beast took Miracle back to his place. The rest of the CIRO group opted, reluctantly, to give them some space. Though they called every day to see how she was doing, Barbie even stopping in to talk to Miracle in private. Beast didn't pry.

A week passed with Beast regulating Miracle to bed. Her bruises were healing and she ached less but Beast was still scared. It was cute at first but after the first day she wanted to scream. She was tired of having him clean her body with a wet wash cloth and orange scented body wash. Saturday close to dinner time, Miracle frowned and climbed out of bed even with Beast protesting.

She made an irritated sound in her throat and

glared at him. "Alric Gerhart! I'm taking a bath today."

Beast kissed her deeply then promised to have something ready for them to eat by the time she got out. But as she stared into the tub, with the water, Miracle found she was glued to where she stood. Just the sight of it caused fear to rise in in her throat, threatening to choke her. She covered her face with her hands, unable to stop the sensation of being held under the water, of the air leaving her lungs and panic set in.

Though she knew she was safe, Miracle couldn't shake off the panic. She sobbed softly while reaching for a towel. After wrapping it around her body, she made her way to the kitchen and waited until Beast turned to her.

"That was a fast...Miracle?" He rushed to her.

Miracle fell into his chest and sobbed harder. His arms circled her as he rubbed her back and kissed her head.

"Tell me what's wrong? What can I do?"

"Can you take a shower with me?" Miracle managed. "I can't...I can't be alone in the water."

"Sure." Beast lifted her head from him so he could see her eyes. "Sure. You should talk to someone."

"Someone?"

"A professional."

"Beast, I'm not crazy."

"I know, *Fleur.* But you've been through something very traumatic. No one expects you to come out of it unscathed and asking for help isn't a weakness." Beast caressed her cheeks with his thumbs. "I'll go with you if you want, but someone who's trained to handle this kind of thing would be better at helping you than me. Please, promise me you'll let me take you to see someone."

"I promise..."

"Okay. Let me turn off the stove and we can get washed up."

This time when Beast took her into the shower, Miracle kept her eyes on him. She refused to look at the tub or the standing shower. She watched him peel his clothes off to expose his gorgeous body. Her eyes dipped to the black bands. "Who did you lose?"

"Lose?" He asked.

Miracle touched the bands around his right forearm.

"Right—their names were Bullet and Soul—short for Soul Train. They were two of the original members of my team. Bullet died in a car accident a year after the team formed. Soul passed away in his sleep two years later."

"I'm sorry."

Beast smiled at her. "Don't be. It was a while ago. Now, it's time to focus on you. Are you ready?"

Miracle nodded. "You told me you were brought up by nuns? What's up with that?"

"My parents died when I was about six," Beast explained, raking his fingers through her hair. "Car accident in India. I had no other family so the government took control of their estate and me."

"Were you ever adopted?"

"No."

"Baby." Miracle sighed. "I'm sorry."

"It's okay. If I had been adopted, I'd probably be a lawyer or something. Then I wouldn't become GSG 9. I wouldn't be a CIRO and I wouldn't have met you."

Miracle blushed. "Aww." She had to kiss him then. "Such a beautiful thing to say. Do you want children?"

"Yes."

"You didn't think about it."

He laughed. "Don't have to. I think I'd be an amazing father."

She kissed his cheek then for she agreed with him.

Beast pulled her towel away and she shivered as his gaze touched her body. But his eyes didn't go hot and sexy as before. Instead, he gritted his teeth and took her hand. Miracle sighed and took a shaky step toward the shower. But the moment she lifted a foot in, she was paralyzed.

"It's okay, Miracle," Beast whispered. "You're safe. You're with me."

Miracle shook her head. "I can't do this."

"Yes, you can. You're strong." Beast kissed the back of her fingers. "I believe in you."

Hearing those words from him, gave her the strength to lift her other foot in, but she wrapped her arms around him and pressed her face into his chest. She felt him shift around until water, the perfect temperature, landed against her back. She gasped and squeezed her eyes closed tighter.

Next was the scent of orange. They'd stopped on their way over to buy a few things she needed but Miracle couldn't concentrate. Instead, Beast picked up everything. The body wash was one of those things. It calmed her as he washed her back, her neck, then lathered her hair. Panic surged through her then but Beast cooed at her softly while sliding his fingers through the wet strands. Those simple actions eased the tension away, and she sighed against him.

He continued working away at her body, massaging her shoulders, her lower back and the spot between her shoulders. When it was time to do her front, Miracle reluctantly leaned away from his body so he could reach between her breasts, over her stomach then between her legs.

He bathed her with care, washed her hair with gentle fingers and once he rinsed her body, he embraced her beneath the water. They kissed, Beast turning his back to the downpour. Miracle suddenly forgot all about what had happened and the fear she felt when it came to water. In that moment, the only important thing was the man with his arms around her, his lips pressed to hers and a swelling of her heart making her want to fly.

When the water ran cold, Beast helped her from the tub, dragged a towel over her to dry her. He stopped long enough to wrap a towel around his hips then carried her to bed. He then disappeared into the bathroom but soon he returned.

"You're wearing too much," Miracle told him.

"It's only a towel. And I thought you may want to rest a little," Beast said.

"No," Miracle said. "You promised."

He bowed his head but the smile he had on his lips couldn't be hidden.

"You're a beast, aren't you?" She teased.

Beast looked at her, a brow arched.

"Prove it." Miracle dared.

CHAPTER 10

Beast rose from the bed and walked over to the dresser. When he returned, Miracle tilted her head to see he held a bottle of lotion. He poured some in a large palm, set the bottle on the bedside table, and met her eyes.

"On your stomach."

"Mmm, yes sir." Miracle shifted to her back as he ordered.

When she did, he surprised her with a back rub, one that turned her to putty. A few places on her body were still tender as a result of her captivity. Each time Beast's strong fingers hit one of those spots she grunted. Beast, this large man who made his living busting through doors, placed tender kisses on her injured flesh. Other than those little hiccups, she relaxed. Beast knew what he was doing —rubbing and kneading and—Miracle whimpered.

"Roll over for me."

Miracle didn't argue, even if she wanted to. Instead, she did as he asked, while he poured more lotion in his palm and rubbed them together. When he touched her again, Beast started from her neck with both hands then spread his palms moving around her breasts and down to her sides. He focused on her breasts, stomach, thighs, down to her feet. His thumbs dug into the soles, making her moan. When he finally made his way back up, it was to spread her open and moved his body between her legs.

Weak and yearning, Miracle pushed to her elbows and watch him. She held her breath, heart racing. He kissed at her stomach, circling the flesh with his tongue as he moved lower and lower. She held her breath until the tip of his tongue found her intimately.

"Mmm."

Beast clung to her thighs, held her in place and teased her with this tongue, sliding it up and down before pulling her tender bud into his mouth. She flopped to the pillows, while holding the back of his head to grind upward onto his tongue.

"You're so good," Miracle panted, sliding her hands up her body, over her breasts then digging her fingers in her hair. He feasted on her until Miracle thought she would lose her mind. Though she managed to hold off her orgasm by breathing hard, Beast didn't want her to do that. He reached up with both hands, cupped her breasts and tweaked her nipples. The floodgates burst open, and she screamed her release.

Beast held unto her as she bucked, caressing her, twisting her nipples and licking at her. When she sighed dreamily, Beast rose up her body to her breasts. By the time he gave both the same attention, Miracle was hot and panting again. He knew what to do to make her react to him, to make her body burn.

"Beast, I've been patient," Miracle whispered. "You're driving me crazy."

"Tell me what you want."

"You."

He smiled down at her. "Be more specific."

She whimpered, wrapped her arms about his neck and pulled his body down against her own. She kissed his shoulder, dragged her lips up his neck before catching his earlobe in her teeth.

Beast growled.

"I want you." She licked it. "*All* of you."

Beast loved the sounds she made for him. Ever since he was old enough to know what love was, he wanted a woman to need him and look at him the way Miracle did. The softness of her voice, the sharp bite of her teeth at his lobe, the smell of her body—all of it mingled together to drive him crazy. Removing his towel, he tossed it over his shoulder and leaned to the side to get a condom from his bedside table. While he did that, he could feel Miracle's hands on his body. She stroked his thighs, his abs, his arousal. It took him a while longer to get the condom—he just couldn't get his mind wrapped around it so he could pick the damn thing. Having her hands on him was the best aphrodisiac in the world.

Then the head of his hardness was enclosed in something tight and wet. He jerked around to see she had moved to her knees and had taken him into her mouth. Beast scooped a handful of condom packets and dumped them on the bed.

"*Fleur*!" He growled. "You don't have...baby."

"You were saying?" She asked him. "Now just enjoy."

Beast met her eyes as she went down on him

again. That was the sexiest thing a woman had ever done to him. She played him like a finely tuned guitar, using her fingers to flow over his abs then dragged her palms down his body to sink her nails into his thighs. He gripped her shoulders and eased her away from him. Miracle was panting, her eyes wild and all he could do was kiss her. He plunged his tongue into her heat, searched and found her tongue. Delirious, Beast wrapped his arm around her and flipped her to her back. He then picked up a condom and handed it over.

She rose to her knees, ripped the pack open with her teeth then pushed the condom between her supple lips. Beast wanted to kiss her again, to feel her mouth on his, to suck her tongue into his—

Miracle bowed forward and used her mouth to slide the condom unto him. Beast held his breath. When he'd first met her he never thought she was this naughty. It wasn't a thing he wanted to change. In fact, he was looking forward to doing this again. He placed her on her back once more and took a position between her thighs.

"This is your last chance to run," Beast said. The moment the words were out his mouth, he knew he'd die if she backed out.

Miracle looked up at him, reached down,

gripped him and pulled the head of his hardness to her entrance. Meeting his gaze, she wiggled her body down until he was halfway into her. Her eyes crossed and that was enough for Beast to give in. He leaned forward, braced himself with both fists on either side of her body. Rooting his knees, he slammed his hips forward.

"Alric!" Miracle screamed.

He took pleasure his name echoing around the room. Miracle was the only woman to make him shiver weakly in her arms. "Scream my name again."

"Mmhmm..." She gyrated against him, meeting each of Beasts thrusts.

She climaxed for him once, twice, three times. He turned her over so she was on her hands and knees then took her again. Each time he pushed into her, her ass jiggled beautifully for him, pushing him into a trance, he didn't think he'd ever want to escape.

The next orgasm to surge through her, got him. He clutched her hips, pushed as deeply into her as he could then helplessly, breathlessly, gave in to the pleasures her body bestowed. For the first time ever, Beast shook violently because of a woman's body. He growled his release for her. "Miracle." He whispered just before slumping to the bed beside her.

Miracle laughed softly and kissed his shoulder. He lifted a weak arm and she eased into his side. Beast smiled. "Miracle...I can never let you go. Please don't take this the wrong way but—" Beast paused a moment to catch his breath. "You're mine."

She blinked at him. "Only if you're mine. I've been through some shitty relationships and they all ended in cheating. I can't go through that again."

He kissed her forehead. "You never have to worry about me straying," Beast said.

"The last man I was with wanted me to lose weight..."

Beast quirked a brow. "Baby, you only lose weight if you want to or if it's affecting your health. I'm happy with your curves, and you ass..."

"Behave yourself!" She smacked him playfully.

"I could." Beast rolled over her, and kissed one of her nipples then the other. He watched as goose-bumps dotted her skin. "But the question is, do you *really* want me to?"

Miracle caught her bottom lip between her teeth and grabbed his ass cheeks. "Not on your life."

"Okay, *Fleur.* Let's have some fun."

CHAPTER 11

The call Miracle had been dreading finally came. CIRO's big boss wanted to talk to them—all of them, Miracle included. While the others went on ahead, Barbie drove Miracle back to her apartment so she could pick up a pant suit and a sensible pair of heels. While she gathered a few things, so she could go back to Beast's apartment afterward, she called Liane to let her know she could come back.

"I'm not coming back, Miracle," Liane said, her voice hard. "I think I'm going back to finish Teacher's College."

"Oh—" That was surprising to Miracle since Liane hated Teacher's College so much she'd dropped out. "What brought this on?"

"Life is short, Miracle," Liane said. "Very short."

"Sure—okay."

"I can't go back to Germany. Please understand."

"It's okay. I'll see you when I come to visit."

"Does this mean things have progressed between you and Beast?"

"Yes." Miracle turned as a knock sounded at the door. Barbie was there tapping her watch. Miracle nodded. "I'll tell you more later. Right now I have to go. His boss wants to talk to us."

"Didn't his boss die?" Liane asked.

"The boss higher than him."

"Oh, okay. Call me later?"

Miracle promised she would and hung up. Barbie walked in and grabbed her packed bag. Though Miracle tried taking it back, Barbie merely grinned and headed out the door. Miracle jogged to catch up.

Back in the car, she slipped on her seatbelt and they were on their way. The two women talked about everything—boys, life, music. The ride wasn't nearly long enough and soon, Barbie fell into a disciplined line with the rest of her team. Miracle wasn't sure what to do so she stood at the door watching them.

The older man with the grey sideburns turned and waved her in. "Please close the door," he said.

Miracle glanced at Beast who nodded and she did as the man asked.

"Have a seat guys," he said. "Miracle Jones, is it?"

"Yes," Miracle replied, not sure if she should say sir, or your highness. Instead she said the one word then sat between Beast and Pitbull.

"My name is Ulrich Weber. I was briefed on what happened to you," Ulrich said. "I cannot begin to tell you how sorry we are."

"I'm still standing—so to speak—I have these guys to thank for helping me out," Miracle said. "They're not in trouble, are they?"

Ulrich smiled. "No. But we are asking you take a vacation. We need to go through the ranks and clean house. We need to know who knew what and when —it's a mess and I really don't want CIRO to be caught in the middle."

"So you're punishing us," Zero said. "We saved a life and you're kicking us out."

"No." Ulrich shook his head. "You've done your job. Now, we have to do ours. Once it's clear, you come back."

"How long will this take?" Beast asked.

"Four, five months? There's no way to tell." Ulrich exhaled loudly. "I don't think I have to tell you this has to stay between us."

"No," Pitbull spoke up. "We got it."

"Who are we going to tell?" Mouth asked. "It would just cause panic. That's why they used cops for GSG 9 and not military. People were afraid something like this would happen."

Ulrich nodded. "I have all your reports. Take the time—we'll pay for it if you want to leave the country for a spell. Once we have everyone vetted, you come back. We won't keep you out longer than necessary. CIRO is one of our more productive teams."

Barbie grunted.

Ulrich dismissed them and they all rose to leave. Ulrich asked to speak with Miracle alone and she saw the moment Beast's back went up. Miracle squeezed his hand and stepped toward Ulrich. Waiting until the door clicked closed behind her, she sighed. The fear of being kidnapped again raged inside her head. Still, she remained standing, keeping her eyes on Ulrich. Beast taught her things and this time she would not be going lightly.

"Is there anything we can do?" Ulrich asked. "This shouldn't have happened."

"I don't think there's anything anyone can do."

"Are you sure?"

"I'm sure. Beast and I..." She stopped.

"Are seeing each other." Ulrich nodded. "He has already made me aware. He's not in any trouble for it. He's a good man, *Fräulein* Jones. Regardless of what's happened of late, we don't make a habit out of punishing good men when great things happen in their lives. Listen, if you ever need anything..."

"I'm sure I won't." Miracle smiled. "I have a group of guys outside that door who have my back."

Ulrich smiled knowingly and nodded. He extended a hand and Miracle shook it.

"Thank you for the offer though," she said.

"The offer is there." Ulrich promised.

With the meeting over, Miracle exited the office to find Beast and the others in deep conversation in the hall. When she approached them, Beast turned to her and arched a brow. She kissed his nose. "It's okay. He just wanted to see if there was anything he could do. I guess he feels guilty too."

"He should." Zero muttered. "He hired the guy."

"You guys have plans for tonight?" Miracle asked.

Everyone shook their heads.

"How about I make you all a good dinner?" Miracle asked. "When was the last time you had a home-cooked meal?"

"Beast?" Mouth asked.

"Look, what the lady wants." Beast wrapped an arm around Miracle's hips. "The lady gets."

The group laughed.

"Perfect." Miracle flailed. "Beast and I have to go shopping."

Beast groaned. "Woman, you are so lucky I adore you."

"You'd better." Miracle joked.

After they set their plans, Beast escorted her to his vehicle and opened her door. She kissed him before sliding into the leather seat. Beast stared in at her for a silent moment before jogging around and easing into the driver's seat.

On their way back to his apartment, he slowed down, measuring his words carefully before speaking. "Have you given any more thoughts to speaking to someone?" Beast asked out of the blue.

"I said I would go and I meant it."

"I know, but sometimes, in the heat of the moment..."

"Beast, I know you're worried about me, and I adore you for it."

"I just want you to be okay." He sighed. "You were kidnapped and tortured. You can't take a shower alone and you haven't taken a bath since it happened. I know why. I can't help you like you deserve and it makes me feel weak. A man isn't supposed to be weak for his woman."

Miracle cradled his face. "Weak? Beast you're the strongest man I know."

"Then why can't I help you?"

She kissed him. "I'll talk to someone," she said. "Because you're right. I love taking baths and it's been torture not being able to have one. Water terrifies me now."

"I'll go with you," Beast said.

"Thanks, hon."

The made it through the night and soon one day rolled into two into three. Miracle visited the therapist. The woman was petite, with blue eyes and dark brown hair. It didn't take a genius to realize the woman was originally a blond. Beast wanted to enter the session with her but she declined. Miracle knew he wasn't good with that but, she couldn't spend the rest of her life afraid of people.

"So, I was told something traumatic happened recently," Doctor Wilhelm said. "Want to tell me about that?"

"I was kidnapped and tortured," Miracle said with a shrug. "My boyfriend believes I need to speak to someone. At first I was upset he'd even suggested it but then he reminded me how I freak out when trying to take a bath. I haven't been able to shower alone since it happened."

"Aquaphobia—you have a fear of water. Any idea why?"

"I was held under water—I almost drowned a few times."

Dr. Wilhelm scribbled in her notes.

And the session continued.

By the end of it, Miracle had to admit, she did feel better.

CHAPTER 12

After three weeks of showering with Beast, Miracle figured it was time to try it solo. When she brought up the suggestion to the therapist, the doctor asked to speak with Beast in private. The meeting hadn't been long and Miracle didn't pry as to what the doctor wanted to know. She figured it was about what to do if Miracle freaked out while in the shower. The first night, Beast sat on the closed toilet seat while she showered with the curtain open. The next time, he sat in the bedroom while she showered with the curtain open. Miracle had panicked both times, but the attacks weren't as paralyzing as the first time she tried taking a bath.

Another week melted by and soon, as long as

Beast was somewhere in the house, Miracle was able to bathe on her own.

One night, as they laid in bed, Beast sat up and faced her. She shifted so she could allow her gaze to travel over his beautifully toned body. His large chest called for her to kiss it all over but his eyes were troubled.

"Miracle, can you do me a favor?" Beast asked.

"Okay?"

"Tell me what happened," Beast said. "While you were kidnapped."

"Why?"

"I need to know."

"Alric." She pushed to her elbow and used her free hand to caress his cheek. "Baby, that wasn't your fault. Your boss gave you an order and you obeyed. You saved a few lives. You can't carry this."

"Please..."

Miracle exhaled and moved so she could curl her legs beneath her. She took his hands in hers and looked down at them before lifting his and kissing the backs. "At first they merely held me in this small room. Then they came for me. They started with knocking me around..." Miracle stopped when Beast flinched. "Beast..."

"I'm okay. Go on."

Though she wasn't sure, Miracle continued. "When I wasn't telling them what they wanted to hear, they tossed me back into the room but came back minutes later. They tried using a hose to spray water into my face. Then they graduated to the tank."

"Did they..." Beast exhaled and cleared his throat. "Did they..."

"No. I wasn't sexually assaulted. If I was, I would have told you immediately and I don't think we'd be able to make love as many times as we have."

"Baby, I'm sorry. I really should have been here for you."

"Like I said, there's nothing to be sorry for. I don't blame you for any of this." She eased in to brush her lips against his Adam's apple. "You're going to want to protect me from everything. But even though your name is Beastmode, it's impossible to save me all the time. Some monsters will be out of control and there will be nothing you can do about them."

"We'll just have to see about that." Beast pouted at her.

Miracle grinned. "I tell you what—we have a little time before we have to get ready for our date. Why don't we find something fun to do?"

"Oh yeah?" Beast leaned in, pressing his large

shoulders into her and taking her lips in short, searing kisses. "I can think of a few things."

"Woohoo!" Miracle cheered.

Beast laughed. "Tell me something—why did your parents name you Miracle?"

"My mom was told she'd never be able to have children," Miracle said. "Then when she got pregnant with me, she was regulated to bed rest for nine months."

"At risk pregnancy?"

"Yes. When I came, apparently the nurse was like, *here's your little miracle.* Maybe it was the pain meds talking but she agreed and *Voila!*"

"Here's my little miracle."

It was Miracle's turn to laugh. "Sure, Beast."

Beast kissed her again and sighed. She wondered if he was okay but she quickly got the answer when she slipped a hand between her legs.

Miracle didn't think making love with Beast could be any better than it had been over the past few weeks. But as he bent her over the side of the bed and took her hard from behind, Miracle realized she had been wrong. He had her rooting back into him as he sunk his fingers in her hair and wrapped the strands around his arm. She panted, whispered his name, mewled for him. All of it seemed to only make him hotter for he throbbed inside her.

"You're so tight." Beast grunted. "How is that...yes *Fleur.*"

Miracle gave in to the wanton vulgarity of what he did to her. She allowed him to pull her hair, and tap her ass with his palm as he drove her from one climax to another with a roll of his skillful hips.

One position morphed into another and when she was on her back, looking up at his sweat drenched body, Miracle took a chance and reached up. She caught his nipples and pinched.

"Miracle, what are you doing to me?" Beast groaned. "Squeeze then harder."

"What's the magic world?" Miracle teased while licking her fingers wet.

"Darling, please..."

With a smile, Miracle caught his tender buds between damp fingers. She twisted and tugged on them until Beast tossed his head back and roared for her. In that moment, he was so damn sexy, she could barely breathe. The look of him, like Poseidon rising from his waves sent tremors through Miracle's body. Just before Beast leaned in to kiss her, her whole body fell apart.

She released his nipples, tangled her arms about

his neck, and surrendered her mouth like she had her body.

Beast looked at himself in the mirror and smiled. He couldn't remember the last time he'd dressed up for anything. Still, there he was, dressed in a black pair of slacks, black Oxfords with matching shirt and leather jacket. The only color in his outfit was a silver necklace with dog tags hanging around his neck. After checking his hair to ensure everything was in place, he added some aftershave to his cheeks and neck. Ready, he picked up the single rose he'd bought for his *Fleur*, along with a small velvet box, he'd been hiding from her.

Hopefully, that would make up for him acting like a jealous idiot. Miracle had to call her professor back in Norfolk about her paper and seeing if she could get an extension because of the recent incidents. She hadn't gotten a hold of him but left a message. He called back and Beast answered after he saw "Kitt Darling" popped up on her screen. He did it because he wanted to know who this man was calling "Darling." How was he supposed to know that was the man's last name?

Needless to say, Miracle hadn't been impressed.

She'd tore a verbal strip off his ass then stormed out. Thankfully, she hadn't stayed gone for long—though to Beast, it felt like an eternity. When she returned, Miracle was much calmer and after a talk and making love, things seemed to have worked out.

It'd been weeks since her kidnapping, and though Miracle was still a little nervous about the water situation, she was still showering alone. They were quick dips—in and out—but was all she needed and he didn't push. When she'd told him what happened while she was in captivity, Beast felt physically ill. If he could kill Loft again, he would—a million times over. Merely thinking of the evil the man put her through riled Beast.

Beast was happy she seemed to show some improvement. With a deep breath, Beast left the bathroom and waited for her in the living room. Her heels clicked against the hardwood floor. He turned and almost fainted when he saw her. He never thought she could look any better to him than she already did. But decked out in a figure hugging black skirt, one of his white shirts, put together with a red neck tie and black stilettos, she had her hair tied up in a simple ponytail, exposing her neck. The only thing that might get in the way of his lips as they searched the warmth of her skin was a pair of dangling earrings, with red rubies at the ends, brushing her ebony shoulders.

Beast realized he hadn't exhaled since he saw her and forced himself to pushed air out his lips. "You look beautiful..."

She twirled for him giving him a perfect view of how the material clung to her ass. He was tempted to postpone the date and take her back into the bedroom, but this was what she wanted. She'd been to a few therapy sessions and her doctor agreed, him taking her on a date would give her a moment to breathe and feel like a woman again. Personally, Beast didn't think she needed his help for that—watching the way she stood before him with poise and perfection told him, she knew.

"Damn..."

"Beast, we have reservations." Miracle kissed his nose. "When we come back, you can do anything you want to me." She winked.

"All I need his half an hour." Beast extended the rose.

Miracle instantly lifted it to her nose. "Then we'll miss our reservation. You bought me a flower?"

"Yes, and you're right. We should go, before I change my mind."

She laughed and turned on her heels for the

door. Beast hung back to watch the way her ass moved beneath the leather of her skirt. "Miracle, before we go..."

"Mmm?" She faced him, lifting the rose to her nose.

Beast held out the long, red velvet box. Her brow shot up.

"Beast...what's this?"

"Open it," Beast said.

When she accepted the box, Beast noticed her hands werenshaking. He held her flower so she could open the box. It'd taken him three days of consistently going to the store to find the perfect necklace. He was pretty sure she'd complain he didn't have to buy her anything but he wanted to. He wanted to have something that every time she looked at it, she would think of him.

When the white gold necklace with a Three-Stone Drop diamond pendant caught her eyes, a tear rolled down Miracle's cheek.

"*Fleur,* I didn't give you a present to make you sad."

She smiled. "They're happy tears. I promise."

Beast lifted the delicate piece of jewelry from the case and stepped behind her. He set it around her neck then let the clasp fall in place. She turned and beamed up at him.

"I love it. Thank you—but I didn't get you a present."

"Trust me, Miracle." He dropped a smooch to her nose. "You've given me more than you can ever imagine. This is just a token to tell you what my intentions are. I want a house overlooking the Rhine and I want that with you."

"Me too."

"Miracle?"

"Mmm?"

"One day, my beauty, I'll tell you I love you—one day very soon."

"And when it happens." Miracle accepted her flower from him again and sniffed it. "On that day, Alric Gerhart, my Beast, I'll tell you I love you too."

The End

ABOUT THE AUTHOR

Kendra Mei Chailyn was born, Kadian Tracey on the small island of Jamaica. She is a multi-published author of interracial, sensual (and sometimes erotic) stories. When not writing, she has a day job or you can find her delving in photography, singing in the shower and trying to adult.

Find Kendra Mei on the Web!

Website: https://kadiantracey.wix.com/romancenorth

Facebook Group:

https://www.facebook.com/groups/meikins/

facebook.com/kendramei.chailyn

amazon.com/Kendra-Mei-Chailyn

bookbub.com/authors/kendra-mei-chailyn

instagram.com/willwryteforfood

twitter.com/kendramechailyn

OTHER BOOKS BY KENDRA MEI CHAILYN

GSG 9 CIRO series

Beast

Barbie

Pitbull

Standalone

Someone Like You

Prey

A Sexy erotic short story

Minor League Alpha: Designated Hitter

Keep in mind Kendra Mei loves hearing from readers! You can find her on the web at https://kadiantracey.wix.com/romancenorth on twitter @kendramechailyn, on Instagram at willwryteforfood and search Kendra Mei Chailyn on Facebook!

Have you seen this child?

Name: Dersim Baran Mahmudi-Azer

Missing since: August 6, 2015

Missing from: Courtney, British Columbia, Canada

If you have information on little Dersim, please contact your local police department.

For more information about missing kids in Canada
and how you can help, please visit:
www.missingkids.ca
https://mcsc.ca

More Books in the Special Forces: Operation Alpha World!

See all the books at www.AcesPress.com

Denise Agnew: Dangerous to Hold

Shauna Allen: Awakening Aubrey

Shauna Allen: Defending Danielle

Shauna Allen: Rescuing Rebekah

Shauna Allen: Saving Scarlett

Shauna Allen: Saving Grace

Brynne Asher: Blackburn

Jennifer Becker: Hiding Catherine

Julia Bright: Saving Lorelei

Victoria Bright: Surviving Savage

Victoria Bright: Going Ghost

Victoria Bright: Jostling Joker

Kendra Mei Chailyn: Beast

Kendra Mei Chailyn: Barbie

Kendra Mei Chailyn : Pitbull

Melissa Kay Clarke: Rescuing Annabeth

Melissa Kay Clarke: Safeguarding Miley

Samantha A. Cole: Handling Haven

Samantha A. Cole: Cheating the Devil

Sue Coletta: Hacked

KaLyn Cooper: Rescuing Melina

Liz Crowe: Marking Mariah
Jordan Dane: Redemption for Avery
Jordan Dane: Fiona's Salvation
Riley Edwards: Protecting Olivia
Riley Edwards: Redeeming Violet
Nicole Flockton: Protecting Maria
Nicole Flockton: Guarding Erin
Nicole Flockton: Guarding Suzie
Nicole Flockton: Guarding Brielle
Casey Hagen: Shielding Nebraska
Casey Hagen: Shielding Harlow
Casey Hagen: Shielding Josie
Desiree Holt: Protecting Maddie
Kathy Ivan: Saving Sarah
Kathy Ivan: Saving Savannah
Kathy Ivan: Saving Stephanie
Jesse Jacobson: Protecting Honor
Jesse Jacobson: Fighting for Honor
Jesse Jacobson: Defending Honor
Jesse Jacobson: Summer Breeze
Silver James: Rescue Moon
Silver James: SEAL Moon
Silver James: Assassin's Moon
Becca Jameson: Saving Sofia
Kate Kinsley: Protecting Ava
Heather Long: Securing Arizona

Heather Long: Guarding Gertrude

Heather Long: Protecting Pilar

Heather Long: Covering Coco

Gennita Low: No Protection

Kirsten Lynn: Joining Forces for Jesse

Margaret Madigan: Bang for the Buck

Margaret Madigan: Buck the System

Margaret Madigan: Jungle Buck

Margaret Madigan: December Chill

Rachel McNeely: The SEAL's Surprise Baby

Rachel McNeely: The SEAL's Surprise Bride

KD Michaels: Saving Laura

KD Michaels: Protecting Shane

Wren Michaels: The Fox & The Hound

Wren Michaels: The Fox & The Hound 2

Wren Michaels: Shadow of Doubt

Wren Michaels: Shift of Fate

Wren Michaels: Steeling His Heart

Kat Mizera: Protecting Bobbi

Mary B Moore: Force Protection

LeTeisha Newton: Protecting Butterfly

LeTeisha Newton: Protecting Goddess

LeTeisha Newton: Protecting Vixen

LeTeisha Newton: Protecting Heartbeat

MJ Nightingale: Protecting Beauty

MJ Nightingale: Betting on Benny

MJ Nightingale: Protecting Secrets
Sarah O'Rourke: Saving Liberty
Debra Parmley: Protecting Pippa
Lainey Reese: Protecting New York
Jenika Snow: Protecting Lily
Jen Talty: Burning Desire
Jen Talty: Burning Kiss
Jen Talty: Burning Skies
Jen Talty: Burning Lies
Megan Vernon: Protecting Us
Megan Vernon: Protecting Earth

As you know, this book included at least one character from Susan Stoker's books. To check out more, see below.

<u>**Delta Force Heroes Series**</u>

Rescuing Rayne (FREE!)

Rescuing Aimee (novella)

Rescuing Emily

Rescuing Harley

Marrying Emily

Rescuing Kassie

Rescuing Bryn

Rescuing Casey

Rescuing Sadie

Rescuing Wendy

Rescuing Mary (Oct 2018)

Rescuing Macie (April 2019)

<u>**Badge of Honor: Texas Heroes Series**</u>

Justice for Mackenzie (FREE!)

Justice for Mickie

Justice for Corrie

Justice for Laine (novella)

Shelter for Elizabeth

Justice for Boone

Shelter for Adeline

Shelter for Sophie

Justice for Erin

Justice for Milena

Shelter for Blythe

Justice for Hope (Sept 2018)

Shelter for Quinn (Feb 2019)

Shelter for Koren (June 2019)

Shelter for Penelope (Oct 2019)

SEAL of Protection Series

Protecting Caroline (FREE!)

Protecting Alabama

Protecting Fiona

Marrying Caroline (novella)

Protecting Summer

Protecting Cheyenne

Protecting Jessyka

Protecting Julie (novella)

Protecting Melody

Protecting the Future

Protecting Kiera (novella)

Protecting Dakota

SEAL of Protection: Legacy Series

Securing Caite (Jan 2019)

Securing Sidney (May 2019)
Securing Piper (Sept 2019)
Securing Zoey (TBA)
Securing Avery (TBA)
Securing Kalee (TBA)

New York Times, *USA Today* and *Wall Street Journal* Bestselling Author Susan Stoker has a heart as big as the state of Texas where she lives, but this all American girl has also spent the last fourteen years living in Missouri, California, Colorado, and Indiana. She's married to a retired Army man who now gets to follow *her* around the country.

She debuted her first series in 2014 and quickly followed that up with the SEAL of Protection Series, which solidified her love of writing and creating stories readers can get lost in.

If you enjoyed this book, or any book, please consider leaving a review. It's appreciated by authors more than you'll know.

www.stokeraces.com
www.AcesPress.com
susan@stokeraces.com

96009252R00092

Made in the USA
Lexington, KY
20 August 2018